Praise for Craig Laurance Gidne

"A town and an art movement arise from a ghostly source in this interesting, hypnotic debut novel from Craig Laurance Gidney. Upon a
grim undercoat drawn from America's shameful histories of slavery
and homophobic oppression, Gidney masterfully layers a centuries-
spanning tale of survival, triumph, and obsession, with a memorable
cast of characters linked by a secret both joyous and frightening. No
simple tale of terror, *A Spectral Hue* enthralls as much as it disturbs."

—Mike Allen, author of *Unseaming*
and *Aftermath of an Industrial Accident*

"*A Spectral Hue* is a subtly disturbing hymn to the joy and terror of
working with a muse, to queer passion and creation, and to the power of art to channel both ancestral voices and personal journeys with
equal intensity."

—Ruthanna Emrys, author of *Winter Tide*

"Craig Laurance Gidney's *A Spectral Hue* pulls you inside its spell,
haunting you, finding its way deep within the folds of your brain. *A
Spectral Hue* paints dark, hallucinogenic colors deep inside your mind."

—John Palisano, Bram Stoker Award-winning author of
Ghost Heart, President of The Horror Writers Association

"In *A Spectral Hue*, Craig Laurence Gidney takes the reader through
multiple centuries via a rotating cast of rich characters to weave an ee-
rily colorful ghost story. The artworks, figuratively and literally haunting, evoke the palpable magic one feels in the presence of such work.
It's all held together by the thread of an enigmatic, influential presence
in the Mid-Atlantic swamp, resulting in a quietly spooky, sometimes
sensual book that is easy to get lost in."

—David Busboom, author of *Nightbird*

Praise for Craig Laurance Gidney's *A Spectral Hue*

"*A Spectral Hue* might just be a horror story—though if it is, I've never read another so full of beauty, found family, and the rapture of art, rather than terror or gore. This novel undertakes to bring the forgotten back into memory, the marginalized into the very center, and all while originating a new and phantasmagoric mythos that is diversely queer and profoundly African American. What a dark and *wonderful* undertaking!"

—Kai Ashante Wilson, author of *A Taste of Honey*

"This is the book we have been waiting for. One of our best short fiction writers finally brings his edgy scary sexy gifts to bear on a novel. A brilliant concept, gorgeously executed. Haunting and unforgettable. Go ahead and give it all the awards right now."

—Sam J. Miller, Nebula Award-winning author of *Blackfish City*

A
SPECTRAL
HUE

A SPECTRAL HUE

CRAIG LAURANCE GIDNEY

WORD HORDE
PETALUMA, CA

First Edition

ISBN: 978-1-939905-50-5

A Word Horde Book
www.wordhorde.com

To the memory of Willa B. Gidney

1: FUCHSIA

She knew the names of everything in the swamp. Every animal and flower. But she did not know her own name. She went through the naming ritual every now and then, hoping that the words would spark some stray memory. Naming things gave them meaning. Surely, she had a name, and there was some meaning as to why she was here, and what she was meant to do.

She spoke aloud. There wasn't anyone else in this landscape of serrated grass and shimmering water. "Larkspur. Foxglove. Phlox. Rose mallow." Speaking the names of things awoke other things. Things that flew, things that swam. "Blue heron. Diamond terrapin. Black duck." The water rippled, things grew. "Paw Paw. Cordgrass. Pond weed."

These words shaped the world. Blue sky, brown-green water. (She didn't say these things aloud). There were some things she knew, the dwindling embers of memory in a pit of ash. She knew that her name was also the name of a flower. How she knew this, she couldn't say. But the knowledge was just there, as was the fact of her sex and the clothes she wore. Sometimes, this frustrated her to no end. She would scream and scream. But no one came. Even the animals didn't startle at her voice. It was useless. Eventually, she sat down on a log or an islet, became statue still. Maybe she even slept a little.

Time stood still here, wherever here was. There was a wrongness about the place. It was a beautiful place. It was a dead place. Birds flew but made no sound. It was neither hot nor cold. Water rippled, but it wasn't wet. And she was never hungry.

Was this Heaven? If so, where was the Lord and the Redeemer? Where were the angels, with their dove-white wings and sun-like halos? She expected a lush garden, where lions laid down with lambs. Where rivers of milk and honey flowed. Maybe she was the only angel here. She wore a long white robe that never got dirty, no matter how deep she waded into the muck. No grass stained her robe, and she emerged from the water dry, the fabric stiff with starch.

She continued her cataloging, sitting cross-legged on a sand islet. "Moth. Water moccasin. Osprey. Cattails. Blue crab…."

***

One day, something changed. The air began to fill with scents. Of salt water, and mud and the tang of algae. Clean smells, mostly, but there was some rot and some sweetness there as well. She put her hand in the dark water. It was cold! There was pressure and humidity in the air, and mist rose from the waters. The woman felt life in the wetlands, life and death.

Was she no longer alone? She couldn't explain it, but she sensed something coming. Someone. Maybe more people, or other things.

She found that the landscape had altered. The grass had more color, sheaves of gold and emerald. Flowers starred the various islets and shores, ruffled and tubular, frilled and ruched, in bright colors winking between the tufts of razor grass.

She herself had altered. She no longer wore the shapeless white robe. She was in a gown as soft and delicate as spider silk spun about her body. It was embroidered like the finest lace.

Best of all, it was the most amazing color. It was the same glorious color as her favorite flower that grew here and there in the marsh. It was a color you sometimes saw in the sky when the sun was setting, staining the clouds. A color not quite pink, not quite purple. Her favorite flower was called the marsh-bell. It was a slender stalk crowned by a perfect sphere of blossoms that hung down in a bell-like fashion.

She saw only one marsh-bell in her timeless time here. A solitary bloom of bright color in all of the watery world. Now, she was the second bloom, in a way.

She wished that more of them grew here, spotting the land from horizon to horizon.

2: XAVIER

"Where, exactly, is Shimmer?" said Dr. Giordano. "I've never heard of it. I like the name, though. It sounds so picturesque. I can see beaches full of dunes and white sand. And old Victorian Painted Houses."

Xavier had promised to text his thesis advisor pictures. But the scene outside of his bus window was bleak. The sky was multiple shades of grey, from ash to slate to coal. And for miles, as far as his eyes could see, marsh wetlands. Algae-laced pools of muddy water were interrupted by patches of reeds, like eruptions of green and brown fur. It was a dismal view. Xavier felt like he was in some post-apocalyptic landscape. In the distance, he saw several raft-like boats sluggishly moving through the landscape. He knew that the town of Shimmer, Maryland was located in the middle of a marsh, not quite an island. But it was one thing to read about it and quite another to see it. And to feel and smell it. Even though the bus windows were closed, the damp, briny scent got in. This side of the Eastern Shore was far from the nicer beach towns of Bethany, Ocean City and Rehoboth.

Shimmer was on the Chesapeake side, where watermen harvested oysters and blue crabs. No one visited this side much. It was bleak and there was a slight chill to the air. It was not worthy of a social

4

media post. *Shimmer,* Xavier thought. *More like Grimmer.*

The fellow passengers on the bus had weathered, ruddy faces and the rough hands of people who worked manual labor jobs. He was the only black person on the bus, with the exception of the bus driver. He also might have been the youngest. Most of the passengers were at least in their late fifties. Furthermore, he was over-dressed, in khakis, a waistcoat with a gold fleur-de-lys pattern and a black long-sleeve shirt. He was suspiciously out of place, a hipster in a bus full of tracksuits and hoodies.

He hadn't known what to expect. There was precious little written about the outsider artists from the small town. Hazel Whitby was the most well-known of the artists. Her quilts were frenzied assemblages of stray fabric, stitched together with her trademark pink thread. Most people thought that they were abstract shapes, and she was heralded as a modernist nearly 150 years before that movement was even born. There was also Shadrach Grayson, with his wild seascape paintings that featured, in the distance, hazily painted blobs of color. There were at least ten to fifteen artists throughout the years. All of them were African-American.

He'd been entranced with the loose movement ever since his undergraduate days, when he came upon a book about African-American quilters. The work of the women of Gee's Bend had so touched him, that he'd began incorporating textiles in his own ab-stract painting. But a brief mention of Whitby's work had led him down a rabbit hole.

Whitby's genius was that she was a master of *trompe l'oeil*. Every viewing revealed something else—a hidden figure, a flower, an eye. Whitby worked primarily with one color palette, the spectrum be-tween purple and pink. Other colors were present in her tapestries, but those shades were centered. Supposedly, she had made hun-dreds of the tapestries. Only thirty of them survived, the rest lost to flood, fire and time.

The bus turned a corner. More salt marsh and waving grasses. Then there was a break in the grey cloud cover. A golden fan of light escaped from the rent, illuminating the landscape. What the light touched was instantly transformed, so that there was a slice of brilliant color in the wan surroundings. The water sparkled, blue and brown, and the grass was a lemony green. Xavier fumbled with his smartphone, and took a couple of pictures before the moment passed. The tear stitched itself together, and the world was plunged once again into misty grey. But for one moment, Xavier could swear he saw, rushing by in a blur, a single flower blooming in the wetlands.

***

62 Crepe Myrtle Terrace was made of dark blue clapboard shingles. The front of the house faced the street, and the backyard ended in a pebbly beach that smelled of algae and old fish. All of the houses on the street were shingled wood, each stained in the camouflage colors of green, brown, and rust. Each of the houses had flat bitumen roofs. Xavier saw flocks of plastic pink flamingos, hordes of garden gnomes, and, in one case, what was clearly a lawn jockey. 62's front yard was mercifully clear of bric-a-brac. There was a neat row of now-dead bushes that were probably forsythias or rhododendrons, and a bird-bath fountain filled with green water.

The door opened, and the woman who stood in front of him was a tiny, African-American woman, and conservatively dressed in dark colors. Black slacks, caramel sweater. She had small hoop earrings, and wore a plum-colored lipstick. Her hair was a close-cropped natural.

"You must be Xavier," she said with a wide smile. Her voice was raspy and warm. She extended a small, delicate hand. "Come in, come in," she said, leading him into her house.

The floors were hardwood, dappled with whorls. They passed through a living room with a large, over-stuffed navy-blue couch and matching love-seats. The furniture sat upon the island of a teal looped rug. The dining room was dominated by a large table, surrounded by sentinel china cabinets. One of them held a service of blue Willowware dishes and wine glasses, and the other was a curio cabinet filled with wood African sculptures, most likely reproductions. Ironwood heads gazed at him. The tablecloth was an indigo and white Ukara textile, patterned with Igbo symbols. The centerpiece was a vase with an arrangement of cloth flowers.

"That's a salt-marsh orchid," Xavier blurted out. When he was excited, he had a hard time keeping his thoughts inside his head.

"Good eye," Iris replied. "In my former life, I used to make and sell cloth flowers. That marsh-bell is a bitch and half to make. But it was my bestseller."

Xavier gently stroked the fake orchid. The flower was a single stalk of dark green from which a sphere full of tubular blossoms drooped down in a conical shape. Most of the tiny blossoms were vivid red violet, but some of them were a gentle mauve color.

"You have to find the right thread color and most of the stores around here lacking."

"You could say, they were 'threadbare.'"

Xavier saw her face move through the various stages of joke revelation. First, the confused wrinkle of the forehead, then the spark of enlightenment, followed by spreading mirth on the features. The laugh, when it erupted, was unlike any laugh he'd heard come out of a real flesh-and-blood human being. It was a cackle. And not just any cackle. It was a cartoon witch's cackle, one that captured Iris's warm rasp. It was so infectious that Xavier felt like laughing, too. He could feel the strain of his face muscles as they gathered up into an involuntary grin.

When Iris stopped laughing, she said, "I just know we'll get along. You have such a corny sense of humor."

"Most of my friends can't stand it."

The tour continued past some shutter doors and into a homey kitchen that could have come out of a 1960s catalog. The refrigerator was harvest gold, which probably once matched the walls, which were now faded to a butter yellow. There were framed posters on the wall: one displayed an imaginary spice rack with illustrations of paprika, cinnamon, oregano and other common seasonings, (it was entitled "Seasonings Greetings") while another had photograph of eggs in a bowl ("Have an Eggs-ellent Day!"). The stainless-steel oven was the only concession to modernity.

"You like coffee? Tea?" Iris said. She hovered near the kitchen counter.

"A cup of coffee would be nice. The bus trip kind of knocked me out."

"Where do you come from?" she said. She rifled through a drawer, and pulled out a bunch of coffee pods with names like Hazelnut Surprise and Donut Shoppe.

"Born and raised in Washington, DC. Um, do you have any unflavored coffee? As strong as you can make it."

She pulled out a pod labeled French Roast and popped it into the machine. She opted for a vanilla latte; the smell was reminiscent of school cafeteria pudding.

"I used to live in Petworth, back in the day. Briefly."

"I live there now," Xavier said. The coffee wasn't bad. It just didn't taste real. It lacked richness. But it was better than nothing.

"Small world," Iris said. She sat across from him. "I hear that DC has changed. It's no longer 'Chocolate City.'"

"That's an understatement. It's more like Artisanal Vanilla City. My neighborhood is overrun with hipsters and the rents are through the roof."

Iris leaned forward, grinning. "Ain't you hipster? I know that you are—what do they call you—a millennium?"

Xavier laughed. "The term is Millennial. And I'm more of a blipster, thank you very much."

Iris let loose one of her witchy cackles.

"So, what brings you to this marsh-side hamlet in the middle of nowhere?" She stroked her coffee mug, which was glazed teal and had the image of a sleeping cat on it. The ceramic cat's tail was so long that it wrapped around the mug like a snake.

"Shimmer is charming," he began carefully. It was one thing to disrespect your hometown (he did it all the time to DC), but it was another thing for an outsider to do it. "But I didn't come here for a vacation."

Iris raised her eyebrow. *Tell me more,* her face said.

"I'm working on my master's thesis," he said, somewhat reluctantly. He hated how pretentious it sounded. As if he were a colonialist anthropologist, studying the natives. "You see, Shimmer was the home of Hazel Whitby and Shadrach Grayson, two African-American artists who—"

"I know about Hazel. She the one that made all of those crazy ass quilts?"

"Yes! Though, I call them tapestries. They weren't really functional, per se."

"Tapestries, quilts. Whatever," said Iris, "those things make me sick, just looking at them. They just seem to move around."

"That's why Hazel's and Shadrach's work is so interesting. Shadrach's paintings also have a decentering effect."

"'Decentering effect.' You talk like a professor. Where you go to school—Howard?"

"No," he replied. "Though my folks wanted me to go. They were both graduates—dentistry and pharmacology. But I got bitten by the art bug, much to their disappointment. I go to an art college in Rhode Island."

"So what are you—a painter? A sculptor?"

Xavier sighed. He hated explaining this part. It was embarrassing, and confusing. "I started out as a painter. Mostly abstract." He saw Iris's eyes glaze over. "But I became interested in writing about art, rather than making it."

"Huh," she said.

***

The second floor had a single runner rug of seafoam green. He glimpsed what he assumed was the master bedroom. The bed was at least queen-sized and had stacks of odd things piled on top of the quilt. He saw a tower of card decks. A couple of bulging quilt-bags were strewn amongst what looked like old coins, and twigs. Iris led him further down the hall, to a room with a door that had peeling paint. Aqua skin, yellow sinew. Xavier felt certain that the room was going to be a dump. Not surprising, since Shimmer wasn't exactly a destination spot.

He was pleasantly surprised by what he saw behind the door. The walls of the room were the color of the sea, a soft greenish blue, while the tufted wool carpet was darker blue in tone, with random loops of yellow and black. The platform bed was dressed in bright white linens, super fluffy pillows and a duvet that just begged to be leapt into. Best of all, the window faced the surrounding marsh. More clouds had broken up, and pools of water sparkled here and there.

"You have a charging station!" said Xavier.

"I'm not uncivilized," said Iris, "even if this is the edge of the world."

***

Xavier unpacked his large suitcase, putting away the sweaters and hoodies he expected to wear during his stay. The air was crisp, cool and damp. He expected days of cloudy, rainy weather. After he put his clothes away, he pulled out his laptop and a couple of library books that were flagged with Post-It notes. He had no real plan, besides visiting the ruins of the house Hazel Whitby, and later, Shadrach Grayson lived in and researching the archives of the local museum. The bulk of Whitby's and Grayson's work was spread out in private collections.

He felt a nerdy glee at the prospect of being close to the physical objects. According to the map function on his smartphone, the Whitby-Grayson Museum was a scant 1/4 mile away. Walking distance. Unfortunately, it had limited hours when it was open to the public. He would have to wait until tomorrow.

The sea-blue room was mostly bare. There was a chest of drawers with a faux antique lamp on the top, a standing cabinet that served as a kind of nightstand, and a large oval full-length mirror. There was a single picture that hung over the bed, a framed blur of pinkish-purple that looked like it was made out of tissue paper.

Xavier walked up to get a better look at the picture. Against a white linen background—perhaps a repurposed handkerchief—a treelike shape was glued together in translucent layers. Beneath the pink opaque shape, and beneath the handkerchief, there was a photograph of something. He turned on the flashlight function of his smartphone, illuminating the picture.

The palimpsest photograph was a picture of the marsh-bell orchid. Iris had said that Hazel Whitby's quilts made her nauseous. She wasn't the only one who thought that. The quilts were riotous things, swirls of clashing colors, and all them referenced, in some shape or form, the marshlands and the orchid.

His advisor, Dr. Paul Giordano, wasn't particularly enamored of Whitby's work. This wasn't surprising. Giordano specialized in the Pop Art and Fluxus movements. He considered Whitby's quilts closer to craft than actual art.

He'd told Xavier, "I know you think she's some sort of visionary artist. I just don't see it. It looks like a mess, to me. Her shapes are uneven, her aesthetic nonexistent. It reminds me of Art Brut—art done by mentally deficient people. Besides, I think it's kind of ugly."

His other committee member, the artist Gilda Devine, had been in the meeting as well. She was tart-tongued on the best of days. "Oh, Paul," she'd said, "I would think you would like ugly art. Isn't that the point of the Fluxus movement?"

Xavier had tried to keep a straight face. It was like watching a play, seeing these two people fight. Paul Giordano was a thin white man with a shaved head, circular John Lennon glasses and always wore paisley shirts. Gilda Devine was an African-American woman, large and muscular, positively Amazonian. She wore loud, batiked wraps and ballet slippers, and her hair was intricately braided.

"Maybe 'ugly' was too harsh a word, Gilda," said Dr. Giordano. "But I find her work, and the work of Shadrach Grayson, for that matter, to be too busy, too frantic. Other than being purple, I don't really see that there's much of a thesis there."

Dr. Devine said, "Don't listen to him, Xavier, honey. Both Whitby and Grayson were likely illiterate and had limited exposure to 'fine art.' They didn't have artistic mission statements. You won't find a thematic continuity that satisfies the Academy." Here, she gave Dr. Giordano one of her laser-sharp glares. "But you will find *something*. I, for one, am excited to see what you come up with!"

***

Dr. Giordano and Dr. Devine were the diametrically opposed influences of his academic studies. Yin and yang, anima/animus.

When he went to Sequoia Arts and Crafts, he'd fully intended to be a painter. His father, Amos Wentworth, wasn't terribly supportive of this decision. Dad was a professor of pharmacology at Howard and made it his life's passion to drive more African-Americans into the STEM fields. His father had no problem with his son painting; it was just not a financially stable career choice. Couldn't he paint on the side?

Berniece Ivy-Wentworth, his mother, encouraged him. She was also a professor at Howard, in the dentistry school. Her younger brother Gideon had been a dancer before he'd died of AIDS in the days before effective drug treatments, and believed that Xavier's artistic nature was a genetic gift. Mom, however, objected to his going to a tiny arts college somewhere in Rhode Island. Howard had a decent studio arts program, and besides, it was free, due to both his folks being assistant professors. It's cold up there, she told him, and only 2.5% African-American.

He sold the both of them on Sequoia Arts and Crafts by telling them that Gilda Devine taught studio arts there. Devine had been recently featured in a *New York Times* article, and at least his mother was impressed.

The move to a tiny town in the middle of a wintry wasteland was difficult for Xavier. The mostly white student population treated him with kid gloves, as if he were a rare hothouse flower. Sometimes, he felt that they only befriended him to prove how 'woke' they were. Dr. Devine, thankfully, took him under her wing.

Not that she was necessarily comforting. She brutally eviscerated his paintings, along with everyone else's. "Naive," "nihilistic," "derivative," "unremarkable" were words hurled at him with some frequency.

She was the one who encouraged him to take more theoretical course work. "Everyone wants to be the next Kara Walker or Jacob Lawrence."

Dr. Giordano joined Sequoia's faculty in Xavier's second year. His art history survey course was multi-disciplinary, multi-vectored and multi-media. He'd use a Bluetooth set and walk up and down classroom rows, wielding his projector remote like a wand. His lectures were full of word play and pop culture references. He managed to link disparate ideas together—queer theory and quantum physics, for example. Or Björk and Francis Bacon. It would make sense, at least at the moment.

Devine and Giordano were frenemies.

Gilda thought that Paul was cocky, more flash than substance. She referred to him as "that little white gay boy," (with affection, of course). Paul had published a couple of art history books that focused on the graphics used by queer activists. His writing style was dense, swirling and confusing, mixing literary criticism, economic theory and historical data. Xavier had to reread several paragraphs multiple times before he could glean any meaning from them. "That little white gay boy tries way too hard," Dr. Devine once confided to Xavier. (He had just nodded noncommittally; but personally thought Giordano's chapter on sans serif fonts as 'anti-heteronormative' was a little too close to poetry than solid scholarship.)

Paul thought that Gilda was too old-school, and that she rested on her laurels. She had made a name for herself in the late seventies with her large abstract palimpsest-style of paintings that captured her crippling migraines. The oil paint was built up thickly, in lumps and bumps, in ugly, bruised colors. Rotten orange, muddy brown, putrid yellow. Some of her paintings had pieces of hair or bits of eggshell embedded in them. All of her work had hidden figures, beneath and behind the thick, scraped coatings of paint. It was violent, unsettling work. Paul, on Gilda's work: "Her retrospective was called 'A Black Girl's Pain.' Really? Why not 'For Colored Girls With Bad Headaches.'"

Both of them weren't in love with Hazel Whitby's quilts, or Shadrach Grayson's seascapes. Giordano had initially shot down the project as "bourgeois mysticism," while Devine thought that there just wasn't enough of a case to be made for the Shimmer Artists.

"It's an art movement made up of Magical Negroes," she'd said to him in one meeting.

(Even now, that barb stung.)

But as he stared at the lone piece of art in his rented room, he couldn't help but feel that it was a sign.

***

Xavier remembered the first time he saw a Hazel Whitby quilt.

He'd been dragged to one of his parents' friends' parties, somewhere in the nearby Virginia suburbs full of McMansions hidden in tree-filled hills. Not ten minutes out of the city, and he saw groundhogs, rabbits, and a doe with a fawn in the falling dusk. He was twelve, and had been told that there would be lots of other kids at the party.

"Maybe you'll make some friends," his mother said. "You never know!"

He *never* made friends at these parties. Mostly, he and the other kids watched as the adults slowly got tipsy and spoke about sports and politics (both national and inter-office). Sometimes, there would be a recreation room with a pool table or foosball table, but he was clumsy when it came to that. There were times when the other kids were all girls, or they were all younger than he was. Or they all went to the same school.

He grunted a response to Mom as they pulled up inside a housing development full of identical-looking houses: all-brick three-story houses with flagstone paths, large front yards, and garages.

Tealights lined the winding front path. He knew that he'd be bored within minutes of entering the house. He hoped that they had good food, at least. Mom was dressed up, in a blue pantsuit with a shimmery see-through chiffon blouse and black sling backs. She smelled of lilac perfume and bergamot hair pomade. Dad was in a suit jacket, lime-green, khakis but no tie. He reeked of Aqua Velva. Within the hour, they'd be smelling of whiskey sours or gin and tonics.

Once they were in the house, Xavier ran the gauntlet of greetings, how-you've-growns, head-tousles and kisses by various women he only vaguely knew. The grown-ups were in a marble-tiled living room, with a full bar and bossa nova blaring from speakers. The kids were sequestered in the basement. This time, the "kids" were all older and furthermore went to various private schools in Virginia. He was the only one from the city itself. There were maybe five of them, and all of their discussion revolved around people they knew. Xavier knew that this would happen. That was why he hated going to parties. At twelve, he could take care of himself.

He drifted away from them, to explore the house. He had to make his own fun somehow. *I could always tell them that I was looking for the bathroom*, he thought, in case anyone asked why he'd escaped the kids' cage. He heard the dull murmur of tipsy adults in the living room when he emerged into the empty kitchen. There was a door out to the main party. Someone was playing a piano. Xavier carefully opened the door. No one was in the hallway that divided the living room from the kitchen. The first floor was colonized by groups of grown-ups, so he dashed up to the second floor.

The master bedroom at the end of the carpeted hall was closed. A guest bedroom, slightly to the left of the stairway, however, was invitingly open. He slipped inside, and partially closed the door so that any patrolling adults wouldn't immediately see him. He clicked on a table lamp, done in the Tiffany style. It was a mushroom cloud of stained glass, with bright purple grapes against a periwinkle background. The lamp's light was feeble against the summer darkness. The room itself was plain, aside from the ornate lamp. The twin bed had a cream-colored duvet and mounds of decorative pillows, like a hotel room. The walls were painted the same beige color as the rest of the house. There was a small bookcase filled with hardcover editions of books by Sidney Sheldon and Danielle Steel. The room reminded Xavier of vanilla ice cream. Not the kind with black pepper-like specks. The kind that was just kind of there, the kind that was sweet and cold and nothing more. Xavier was about to turn off the lamp and explore other rooms when something caught his eye.

At first, he thought it was a poster of a particularly ugly abstract painting. The colors clashed, and the shapes were crudely drawn. But, it wasn't a print. There was too much texture there, lumps and bumps, like an old pillow. Threads hung down, undone. Xavier went up to the wall hanging. It wasn't a painting at all. It was some kind of quilt that had been mounted and sealed behind glass. In the weak light, he couldn't make out what he was supposed to be seeing. He switched on the overhead light. He didn't intend to stay long in the guest room. But turning on the light brought the quilt to life.

Purples and blues, greens and browns all surged together in a kaleidoscopic fashion. Dots of purple-pink scattered across the piece. Stitches divided chunks of green and blue.

Xavier stepped closer to the quilt, beguiled. He found that if he stared at it long enough, it began to move. At first, he thought it was just spots before his eyes, due to the sudden flood of light. But the purple-pink flecks moved, zooming back in and out of the tapestry. And, in moving, they revealed more about the tapestry's intention. The blue fabric, which shimmered like satin, was supposed to be water. And the daubs of green were grass. Little islands in a mostly still waterscape. At the top of the tapestry, there were brownish green smudges, the suggestion of trees. What were the specks of magenta meant to be, then? He watched as they luminously hovered about in the grassy clumps and over the water. Somehow, he knew that it was salt water. He could even smell the brine, as if the quilt had been dipped in there.

"There you are!" He heard his mother's voice. It was jarring enough to stop the dance of the pink-purple specks. "He's in here, Amos."

It took effort to pull his eyes away from that woven marsh. When he did, he found himself in the guest room, with his parents staring at him from the doorway. For the briefest of moments, the purple-pink sparks were superimposed against the room, as if the tapestry were projecting images. Xavier blinked them away.

"Have you been here all this time?" Dad asked him. "We were looking for you downstairs."

"We thought you'd wandered off," his mother added.

Were they worried? His mother's voice had a frantic edge to it, and Dad sounded annoyed.

"You know better than to go creeping off in people's houses," said Dad.

"I'm just glad he's safe. Come on, honey, it's time to go." Mom made some ushering movements with her hands. Time to go. *How long had he been in the room?* He thought that approximately fifteen minutes had passed since they'd arrived at the Bairds. A half-hour at the most. Had something bad happened? Was that why they were rushing out?

"Look at the tapestry, Mom. Dad," he said. "Isn't it cool?"

He heard a female voice behind his parents. "It's an original Hazel Whitby piece."

"It's a what?" his mother muttered.

Mrs. "Edyie" Baird swanned into the room, shoving his parents aside. She was dressed in a white pantsuit. A golden-faced sun medallion dangled between her décotellage, and she wore a large turban, hiding all of her hair. Mrs. Baird *always* wore turbans. When he was younger, he'd told his mother that she looked like a genie. His father wondered if there was even any hair beneath her neverending supply of hats. ("She might be as bald as that Sea Hag on Popeye," his dad once said.)

"Hazel Whitby," said Mrs. Baird. "She was a former slave who lived on the Eastern Shore. She made hundreds of quilts. Even inspired other black artists. I believe they started a mini-movement."

Dad said, "Huh." Which meant that he thought that quilt wasn't much to look at. Mom had that glassy-eyed look that indicated that she wasn't really interested.

Mrs. Baird continued: "They are very collectible. Some of them are even in art galleries."

"You don't say," Mom replied. She examined the tapestry, her face scowling up in concentration.

"I had it appraised. I got it for two-fifty. It's worth two thousand."

"It is certainly *colorful*."

"The purple spots move," Xavier said.

"The colors do clash," Dad said. "But, it's getting late. We're the last ones here, and I'm sure that Edyie and Aaron would like to rest after giving such a grand party."

Mrs. Baird insisted that it was no trouble at all. On the ride back home, he almost fell asleep to his parent's gossipy banter. How So-and-So got drunk, and Mrs. Whoever was always putting on airs. He closed his eyes. Then he heard his parents talk about Mrs. Baird.

"Edyie has some bold taste," Dad said.

Mom said, "What you mean?"

"Those Ali Baba turbans."

"You know she has alopecia. I think she's made lemonade out of lemons."

"All right, all right. But that quilt she had was *ugly*. She got it for two-fifty, and it's worth two thousand?"

"You think she's lying? I don't. Edyie knows her stuff. She used to work down at the Smithsonian."

"As a *secretary!*"

"Still. She has a good eye. And not all art is supposed to be pretty."

"Apparently," said Dad, his voice dripping with sarcasm. Mom laughed.

Xavier kept his eyes closed, but his mind was racing. Did no one else see the moving spots of pink-purple flame? And how long had he been staring at the tapestry?

3: IRIS

When Iris Marie Broome drove past the Whitby-Grayson museum, her shoulders tensed up. For the most part, she avoided the place but there was no other way to get to Winslow's Bakery. The AirBnB venture was a new chapter in her life, and she wanted to celebrate the milestone with a Smith Island cake, a regional specialty. She no longer worked at the hospital gift shop a few towns over and she had gotten a nice windfall from Tamar's estate. She'd been finally able to afford the boxy slate gray Kia she now drove. It was used but barely driven. Most of the cars she had had were on the verge of collapse in one way or another. As it trundled past the museum, Iris saw nothing out of the ordinary. Just the closed building and surrounding wooden planters full of marsh-bells.

She unconsciously relaxed, her teeth unclenching, the knot in her shoulder unraveling. She got to Winslow's just under the wire: it was fifteen minutes to closing. She felt a pang of elation—there was one whole cake left. Smith Island cakes were that odd blend of homey and elaborate. Each cake had at least seven layers of moist but stolid yellow cake. It was smothered with its trademark boiled ganache icing. This was a delicious but proudly unfancy confection, a favorite treat for watermen because the fudgy boiled icing held its shape in the harsh salt air.

"What's the occasion?" asked Jen Winslow as she boxed up the cake. Iris always liked Jen. She'd always made a point to be gracious to her and Tamar, and treated them like old friends. Adjusting to the remote town had been difficult for the both of them. Shimmer was tiny, and the townsfolk, many of whom came from a long line of Shimmerites, were slow to warm to new people. The fact that Iris and Tamar were together didn't help matters. But Jen didn't care. Tamar thought that she was closeted: "Remember when she talked about how much she loved the movie *Fried Green Tomatoes*? She asked me, 'Were those two girls in love or what?'" Iris didn't think that was enough evidence.

"I'm not working at the hospital anymore," said Iris. "I hated that job anyway. You had to stand up all the time, even when no one came inside. No more hour-long commutes."

"Hallelujah," said Jen. "Though any day is a great day for cake."

"Girl, I'm not gonna eat it myself. Though I could. I've started doing the AirBnB thing. You know, renting out my room like an apartment. I have all of that house to myself...." She didn't finish the sentence. She had drifted into awkward territory. Iris could see the pity beginning to write itself across Jen's features. "I have my first guest. He's a student studying Shimmer's history."

"It'll be a short book," Jen said with a laugh. "More like a pamphlet."

Iris smiled at Jen. She wasn't bad looking, with a face as round as a full moon, smooth skin and braided hair extensions that were threaded with cobalt blue. Maybe Tamar was right about Jen.

I should ask her out to a movie sometime, she thought. Ever since Tamar had died, Iris had become a bit of a hermit.

She picked up the cake box, and started for the door. She almost dropped the cake, which would have been a tragedy. She was startled by what she saw next to her car.

There was a ripple of color there, somewhere between a heat mirage and the scintillating play of light on a stream. A scattershot speckle of pink light gently undulated into and out of existence. The light was the color of cherry blossoms. The translucent shape that housed the phenomenon was the rough outline of a person. She couldn't determine anything specific about the apparition, no features or gender. It was just random flashes of pale pink.

Not again, thought Iris.

"Is everything okay?" Jen's voice broke her trance.

"Yes," she said. She knew that she didn't sound convincing.

The wavering apparition didn't move from the side of her car when she approached it. Iris put the cake in the backseat, and after a quick glance to see if anyone was watching, she whispered, "What do you want to show me?"

She waited a beat. Then the pink translucence faded away.

***

"You should go into business," Tamar told her many times. "If Miss Cleo can make money that way, so can you."

And Iris always replied, "Why? It's not like I can really communicate with them."

They called them 'caspers.' The caspers were beautiful, abstract things, like floating scarves or specks of light. They were in many colors, and sometimes they were also textures. Often they had the shape of a person, but not always. Iris just saw them. When she tried to interact with them, all she got was a stream of nonsensical images in flashes. One casper might send her a collection of shells, a hair comb, the face of a silver tabby, a beach scene. Another would flash a silver jewelry box, an old 45 single, and a discolored flower flattened between book pages. It was a hodgepodge, what she saw, with no logic. Iris trained herself to unsee the tattered caspers, who, for the most part, seemed oblivious. None of them could manifest completely, and they seemed to be unmoored and confused. This was especially true of the sightings at the hospital. When she wandered away from the gift shop, the dead filled the lobby and the various floors she visited to deliver floral arrangements and balloons. She saw the shredded and portioned silhouettes of the recently dead roaming the halls—half a woman the color of eggshells, a man seemingly made of shiny black vinyl. And sometimes, children in pastel tones.

"You could try communicating with them through, I don't know, a Ouija board," Tamar said. She bought a board from a nearby big box store, and one night, they tried it. They contacted a couple of folks: a man named Callum and a person of indeterminate gender named Dion. (One of the questions they had asked, "Are you female?" The planchette slid to both Yes and No.)

When that didn't work, Tamar bought a deck of tarot cards, along with a book that explained the various spreads that could be used to summon and interact with the deceased. Iris never had the time to sit down and study the fairly complicated symbolic code. The deck that Tamar purchased, though, was interesting. It had an Afrocentric theme, with many of the major arcana represented by Orishas. She remembered that Oya was the Empress and Eshu was the Fool. Despite that, she didn't care for the tarot deck. There was one card, the High Priestess, that Iris found disturbing, though she didn't tell Tamar for some reason. The dreadlocked woman centered in the midst of darkness wore a wrap of glowing fuchsia, a color that was replicated in the highlights of her eyes. It was one of those pictures where the eyes followed you wherever you went. Iris hated pictures like that. Furthermore, no other figures—not the Hermit or the Hanged Man or the Hierophant—were depicted with such detail or in lurid colors.

When she got home and put away the cake, she went into her

bedroom. She was in the process of downsizing, getting rid of the detritus of Tamar's things.

"I wonder why she came for me," Tamar said. *"You were more a fit for her."*

She brushed that thought aside, as if it were a gnat. Tamar's face flashed in her mind. And her voice—what did it sound like, again? She had the sudden urge to listen to her voice, its honeyed soprano. But she didn't have a recording of it. Iris tamped down the feeling, and continued sorting out the mess on her bed.

There were books on numerology and the zodiac.

"You're a Scorpio, aren't you?" Tamar had said when they first met. *She had been wearing a silk green dress and had a white gardenia in her hair.*

"How can you tell?" Iris asked her. She hadn't said two words to the new hostess.

Tamar waggled her eyes. "It's a gift I have."

Iris moved the books into the Donate pile. There was a Goodwill in Bethany Beach. They took everything.

Tamar also went through a crystal phase. She left behind a jewelry box full of agates, rose quartz and tourmalines.

"Do you feel any energy from the stones when you handle them?" she asked Iris.

"They just feel like rocks, babe. Sorry."

Iris picked up some of the crystals, and sifted them through her hands. She liked the sound of their clicking together, and the cool, smooth texture against her skin. The pink quartz, though, reminded her of the disembodied entity she had seen in the parking lot.

She remembered Tamar, sweating and disheveled, bent over a table strewn with tissue paper and varnish and the cuttings from wallpaper sample books and magazines.

"I feel her moving through me. I am her vessel."

Iris sat down on the bed. It had been five years since she'd last seen

Tamar. And only one year since she learned that she had died. Aunt Hagar had been vague about the cause of her death, but deep down inside, Iris knew Tamar had killed herself. When she saw the waxen body in the coffin, she was enraged. She knew that Tamar wanted to be cremated, and her ashes scattered in the Shimmer Marsh. Though they were not together—Tamar had moved to Oakland to live with her aunt—they still emailed and later texted, and even sexted. It was like they were together, if only in an abstract sense.

Cherry blossom pink had been the color of spirit she had seen outside of Winslow's. A pale delicate color that wasn't the glaring magenta color of the marsh-bell.

Iris hated that color.

***

Iris was eleven years old when she began seeing auras. She could remember the first one she saw.

Aunt Earline appeared as suddenly as Mary Poppins when her grandfather began getting ill. She didn't even know that she *had* an Aunt Earline until one rainy day in April she showed up on the doorstep of the rowhouse in Philly. It had always been just her mother, Mona, and her grandfather. Iris's father had died when she was very young. The week before, Pop-Pop, her grandfather, had had his foot amputated, so she had thought the burly woman in an orange dashiki was some sort of weirdly dressed health aide. She was tall, maybe the tallest woman she'd ever seen, and what Pop-Pop would refer to as "big-boned."

"Hey, Iris," the woman said. She knew her name, somehow. "How's it hanging? I've been dying to meet you."

In that moment, Iris knew that this woman was somehow related to her. She could see the reddish tint to her perfectly round Afro, the constellation of dark freckles over her light skin. She even had similar features to Pop-Pop, the same lip-shape, the same deep-set eyes as her mother. Relatives had come "out of the woodwork" after Pop-Pop's surgery. Relations from Pittsburgh, Mechanicsville and Baltimore, bearing terrible looking casseroles and molded gelatin salads. All of the women had -ine and -ette names. She could never get them straight. Georgette. Pauline. Marvine. Harriet. They bought along their bored husbands, their surly teenaged kids, and fussed about Pop-Pop's bed, fluffing pillows every two minutes or so. At least this one didn't have a gross heat-n-serve dish.

"I'm Earline. Your aunt." She stepped into the narrow vestibule, which could barely contain her girth. All of the -ines and -ettes were presented to her as "aunts," so this designation meant nothing to her. She moved aside, to let her into the barely wider front hallway.

"Mama," Iris yelled up the stairs, "Aunt Earline is here."

Her mother emerged from Pop-Pop's sick room, at the top of the stairs. The look on Mom's face was shock. She looked as if she had just seen a ghost.

"Mona," said Aunt Earline. "You haven't changed a bit."

The shocked look on Mom's face fell away. It was replaced by another, darker emotion. She quickly shut the door to Pop-Pop's room and came down the stairs. Her eyes were narrowed. "So you finally showed up," she said. "I don't believe it."

"I had to come," said Earline. "I mean, 'honor thy parents' is in the top ten, ain't it?"

"Who told you about Daddy?" her mother said.

Iris, standing between them, thought for a second, *Who's Daddy?* And that's when it clicked into place. The two women had the same 'high yellow' skin tone and reddish-brown freckles on their faces. But they were complete opposites. Mom was small, not even five feet, while Earline towered over her. Mom looked like a doll next to Earline. A doll in a stiff grey dress, with white stockings and matching grey pumps. The only jewelry she wore was a simple silver cross necklace. Next to Earline's loud outfit, Mom looked like a nun.

"Suzette called me, and let me know."

"Suzette? Suzette, down in DC? How did she even know how to contact you?"

"It's a long story," said Earline. "And I've been traveling all day to get here. Plane, train, bus. I'd like to see Daddy, if you don't mind."

"He's sleeping now," Mom said. Her voice was lowered, her expression slightly less stony. "We can talk about it in the kitchen."

She ushered them into the room at the back of the house, with its walls the color of pale butter and the round white Formica table in the center. The countertop was covered with a couple of cakes and pies, hidden beneath domes. Mom set the kettle on to boil.

"Aunt Georgette brought your favorite," said Mom.

"Mincemeat pie?" Earline's voice, which was deep, went up a few octaves.

Iris stared at the slice Mom placed before Earline in abject horror. The crust was invitingly flaky, but the filling was brown and ambiguous. A kind of gelled gravy enrobed chunks of something or other. The 'minced meat.' A strange, sweet and boozy smell wafted up. Earline closed her eyes in pleasure at the first bite, murmured an "mmmm."

For briefest of moments, a lacy veil, the color of the early morning sky, enveloped Earline. It unfurled with each savoring bite of the mincemeat pie. Iris gasped. Was it a mist? A light? A piece of fabric?

Mom said, "Something wrong, Rissy?"

But the whatever-it-was retreated, glowered about Earline's shape, a shimmering blue outline.

"Nothing," she said cautiously.

Earline finished the pie, started on the coffee that Mom had made for her. "That sure was good. Child, it's so nice to eat real food again. I will retch if I have to eat another alfalfa sprout again."

"Does this mean that you're out of that group?" Mom stood, leaning against the counter.

"Black Gnosis is no more," Earline said.

"And we don't have to call you Sister Imani?"

"Sister Imani has left the building."

"What are you all talking about?" Iris couldn't stand it any longer.

Earline gave Iris the once-over look. "You don't know? They didn't tell you?"

"Tell me what?"

"Well, when you were two, and your daddy was still alive, I joined a religious group called Black Gnosis."

"Religious group," Mom muttered, "more like cult."

"Now, now, Mona. I'm not disagreeing with you. But let me tell the child the story my way."

Nine years ago, Mona and Lamar Broome lived a few blocks away, in an apartment building. Iris had no memory of the apartment but apparently she'd spent the first two years of life there. Earline still lived at home with Pop-Pop. She was a year older than Mona, and was, in her own words, "a lost child."

"A hot mess," Mom said under her breath. Iris thought, *Mom really hates her sister.* That's when she saw the thin outline of color surrounding her mother. Earline's had been clear blue. The light emanating from Mom was a muddy red color, like an old bloodstain that refused to come out in the wash.

"Your mom isn't wrong," said Earline. "I *was* a hot mess. A lost soul, stumbling through life. After Mona married Lamar and left the house, I started up secretarial school cause Momma—your grandma—said single girls could meet men out in the workforce. But I never got the hang of shorthand and dictation. I might as well learned a new language. When Momma got ill, I quit school to help around the house."

"What did Grandma die of?" Iris asked. Both her grandfather and mother were tight-lipped about things like death and illness.

"Rissy!" her mother hissed, as if on cue.

Earline: "You didn't tell her? I swear. It's nothing to be ashamed of. Momma died of stomach cancer."

Iris watched her mother actually flinch at the naming of the disease. As if saying 'cancer' could summon those rotting cells. Her halo-light deepened in color, became bloodier.

"It's not like *you* had to take care of her," Earline said.

"You know that Iris was born around that time. I couldn't—"

"Chill, sis, chill. I'm not blaming you. Anyway. When Momma passed—"

"Bless her soul," said Mom.

"We all went nuts in different ways. Daddy became a holy-roller. He read the Bible backwards and forwards, went to services on Wednesday and Sunday. Started quoting the Good Book in every situation. Corinthians this, Leviticus that."

Pop-Pop was still a 'holy-roller.' (Iris liked that phrase; she imagined a steamroller the color of the Golden Calf trundling down the streets, flattening sinners on the pavement.) She wasn't allowed to listen to secular music. He'd warned her of the Satanic messages hidden in rock music, and how they could summon demons. (She doubted that 'Boogie Oogie Oogie' was some witch's spell when he'd told her that.)

"It was during this time that I met David Okeke, the leader of Black Gnosis. He was one charismatic dude. And he looked a little like Sly Stone. He knew several languages fluently, and he knew the Bible as well as Pop-Pop ever did."

"Oh, hush," said Mona. "Daddy reads from the Good Book every night."

Earline paused, and rolled her eyes at her sister. "Daddy knows the King James Version. Does he know the original translations from Ancient Greek and Latin? Does he have a copy of the Apocrypha, the books of the Bible that were edited out by King James? Well, David Okeke did."

Mona finally deigned to take a seat at the white round table. "Black Gnosis is a heathen cult. They worship African gods alongside Christian ones. Who's that goddess you worship who wears pink?"

"We only worship the one true God, and his son, Yeshua. Black Gnosis is a Christian group. The goddess in pink, as you call her, is the mother of Yeshua. She is the feminine divine, the black avatar of the Gnostic Sophia, Christian goddess of wisdom and secret knowledge."

Mom looked like she was going to have a fit. "That's blasphemy," she said, through gritted teeth.

"Technically, it's heresy," Earline replied. "But, it's not even that…"

The two sisters began to argue in earnest. Earline was easy-going, and didn't take it seriously. This drove her mother crazy. Mona was a daddy's girl, through and through. Earline probably took after Ethel, the grandmother Iris had never met. Iris stopped paying attention to the minutiae of the sisterly spat, picking out things that sounded interesting. Iris was in the midst of a passion for anything pink. All of her favorite shirts, and hair accessories and socks and scarves, were some shade of that color. She was intrigued by the idea of a goddess that wore pink things.

Meanwhile, the halo-lights of the two women began flashing like strobe lights. Moody blue, muddy red. It began to bother her, so Iris left the women to their quarrelling. She snuck upstairs, and paused by Pop-Pop's room. It smelled of sickness: astringent medicines masking sweet rot. Pop-Pop was asleep, his eyes moving rapidly beneath their closed lids. His breathing was shallow and rough and there was a sheen of sweat on his brow. But that wasn't all that Iris saw. A translucent, wispy shawl of black, lightly spangled with red, hovered over his body.

Instinctually, Iris knew what the black shawl meant, as it translucently hovered over her grandfather. It meant imminent death. She resisted the urge to lift up the edge of the comforter that hid his amputated foot. It was too macabre. The medical term for the rotting flesh was gangrene. (For the longest time, Iris thought her mother was saying Gang Green. She imagined a microscopic army of sickly green cells, eating away at Pop-Pop's foot.)

The shawl encased his body like a filmy web. He looked like a mummy. Iris was in the room before she knew what she was doing. She began waving the black shawl away. It dispersed briefly, into shreds and tatters, before it coalesced back together. Iris snatched at it again. It was a pointless exercise. Death would not leave its web. She wished she had scissors, to rend the veil into a thousand tiny pieces.

She snatched up a bunch of the black stuff. It was a cloud, wet and vaporous. It also stung, like wires or nettles. It squirmed between her fingers, flowed through them. It was an ugly color. Not a rich, luminous black, like the hair on her head or the space between the stars. No. It was grey-black, faded and unhealthy looking. Why couldn't the shawl that covered her grandfather be a better color, something more vibrant. More alive. Not this half-color that leached the life out of him. Something bright. Something pink, like the wisdom goddess that Earline spoke about.

It didn't happen immediately. It was insidious, slow, but the grey threads of transparent shawl began to change. Grey into pearl. Pearl into peach, like the inside of a shell. The threads were few and far between, yet they were brighter than the formless mass of the death-shawl.

"Rissy! What are you doing in here!"

She dropped the piece of cloud at the harsh sound of her mother's voice.

"Take a chill pill, Mona," said Aunt Earline.

"I expressly told you not to disturb Pop-Pop. He needs his rest." By this time, Mom had her French-tipped nails on her shoulders, piercing through the thin fabric of her blouse.

"Leave the child alone," said Earline. "She's hardly in the damned room. I see you're an old school style parent."

Mom let her go, and faced Earline. "How dare you. How dare you judge me. You have no idea what it's like to raise children."

"Actually, I do." Earline was calm, cucumber-cool. "Black Gnosis ran several day care programs in Oakland and Detroit. I've worked with children of all ages. And I know that spare-the-rod crap doesn't work."

Mom was speechless. Her mouth hung open. Iris could feel the tension in the air. The pressure dropped. And Mom's blank expression hid the roiling anger within her. Iris wished she could warn her brand-new aunt about the tongue-lashing she was about to receive.

The impending fight, though, was defused.

"Mona?" came Pop-Pop's dry voice. Iris heard cracked earth in those tones. His voice was shriveled, like a raisin.

"Daddy," she said. Iris knew from experience that the fight was far from over. It was just delayed. Mom could hold grudges. "How are you doing? Do you need any water? Are you too warm?"

Pop-Pop grunted, waving away her questions. "Who's that in the doorway?"

"It's me, Daddy," Aunt Earline said. Her voice was suddenly timid. Iris noted that Earline didn't move away from the door frame. "I've come home."

Pop-Pop weakly motioned both Iris and her mother to move aside. His hands trembled. "Earline?" he said. It was a choked whisper.

"Yes," Earline replied.

Then Pop-Pop did the strangest thing, as strange, in its own way, as the shawl-aura things Iris saw.

He began to cry. His wrinkled face became even more wrinkled. Large tears leaked from behind his glasses, the streaks getting caught in the folds of flesh. His lips quivered. Iris was stunned into silence. Pop-Pop never cried, not even when he lost his foot. She didn't even think he had the ability to cry.

Mom said, "See what you've done? You went and upset him."

"Oh, Mona. Hush," Earline said as she moved into the room. She went to Pop-Pop's bedside, and embraced him. He looked so small and frail in her giant arms. The translucent shawl draped itself over her arms, enfolding her grandfather. The black halo around him changed color, to a light, spring-like green. The green of pistachios, mint, and new leaves. Pop-Pop trembled like a baby in Earline's arms.

***

It was nice to have someone else in the house. She had been used to living alone for so long that she had forgotten how nice it was to see someone in the morning and the evening. Xavier mostly kept to himself, bouncing between his room and the museum, but they shared breakfast and dinner together. The past few years, Iris had become a hermit. Her mother and her aunt had passed just before Tamar left. She'd spent hours going through dead women's things, and dealing with probate courts in Pennsylvania. Mama's stuff had been easy to get rid of; it was mostly clothing her mother hadn't updated since the '80s and '90s, an endless supply of garish colors and shoulder pads. And church hats. Mama's hats were architectural wonders, with sombrero-wide brims and gardens of fake flowers. The only thing she kept of Mama's were the photo albums. Aunt Earline was used to living frugally, so there wasn't much to get. Iris ended up with her collection of masks and sculptures. They now hung in her bedroom. These stylized wooden faces were sometimes her only company for days on end. She still had a bunch of Tamar's things, stuff that Tamar had left in Shimmer.

Xavier left for the museum every day at 9:45am. It was a brisk fifteen-minute walk there and the weather was cooperating so far. She'd been tempted to drive him there the first time, just to get his bearings in the small town.

Then, she thought about the pink translucence she'd seen. She hadn't seen any caspers for quite a while, and it was strange that it showed up in broad daylight. She knew that she should be used to them by now. But, the thing had followed her. Waited for her.

The sound of a phone ringing broke into her reverie. The ringtone sounded like cricket chirps, and it came from Xavier's room. Iris knew that he had left for the day, so he'd probably left the phone by mistake. She entered his room, and found the small phone still plugged in, with a "Mom called" message on the screen before it faded away.

She sighed. The right thing to do would be to take the phone and charger to him.

***

"Is Xavier Wentworth here?" Iris asked the man behind the information desk. He towered over her. If she hazarded a guess, he was maybe six-foot-five and rail-thin. He wore a grey coverall with the name LINCOLN sewn in a white oval. Lincoln hunched his shoulders as if he were ashamed of his height.

"Yes, he's in the back. Shall I get him?" Lincoln avoided eye contact, as if he were distracted.

"He left his phone at my house," Iris said, "and I'd like to hand it back to him."

The tall man nodded and left. Iris stared at the desk, with its computer monitor, its metal form curved in a U shape and topped with a glass ledge.

Don't look at the walls. Don't look at the walls.

The information desk was stacked with brochures. Brochures that had reproductions of the art on high gloss paper.

That was all it took.

She stood in the marsh. It both was and was not the Shimmer Marsh. From horizon to horizon, islets full of reeds stretched. There was no tree-line. Only water, in shades of blue and streaked with chalcedony-green blooms of algae. The marsh floor was fawn and chocolate, dusted with traces of white and grey silt, strewn with broken shells and fish bones. The colors were super-saturated, like a painting. The color here wavered, echoed and sang. They were more than just strands of light, filtered through a prismatic lens. Iris felt each color as an emotion. Mournful blue, resilient green, cheerful yellow. Marsh-bells dotted each clump of grass, vibrating delirious euphoria like a note just beyond hearing range. For a moment, she let it wash over her.

I've missed this.

It was glorious, this feeling of belonging and joy.

A marsh-bell sphere expanded next to her, the blossoms fusing together like glass. The stem sank, and the muddy ground grew. The blossoms came together, became a fabric satiny in its sheen. In the whirlwind of bright purple, arms and legs grew. The veil parted, revealing a face. Or, something like a face. Eyes were the beads of stamens, the mouth was the trumpet of a blossom.

Iris, it said.

With Tamar's voice.

"Iris?"

The dream marsh burned away, replaced by sealed concrete, cinderblocks, fluorescent lights and the face of Xavier in front of her.

His face was wrinkled with concern.

She felt a moment's embarrassment at her spaciness, followed by anger, at herself, for coming here in the first place.

"You left your phone," she said, when she got her voice back. She fumbled in her purse, pulling out the phone and the charger.

"You okay?" He took them from her hands.

"Oh, it's nothing," Iris said. "Just fluorescent lights give me headaches." She shaded her eyes, as if to demonstrate.

That seemed to quell his concern. "Thanks so much," he said.

It took all of her resolve not to dash to the museum entrance.

4: LINCOLN

The Bayside Motel was the type of place that was probably rundown even when it was new. It was a motor-court style establishment, with a moat of cracked black pavement and parking pylons. In the middle of the sea of black, there was a raised concrete platform that fenced in a kidney-shaped pool that was currently empty and clogged with dead leaves and cigarette butts. The roadside neon sign was remarkably intact. Only the 'O' in motel was burned out. The sign was animated with three pink starfish and an aqua blue seahorse.

Lincoln had stayed in worse flophouses. There were not a lot of cars parked in front of the rooms, and the Vacancy sign flared hot red.

The motel was a two-story rectangle of white stucco and drab green doors. The office/lobby was on the left side, nearest the roadside sign. The inside of the office was drab, with vinyl furniture, cracked tiles and dusty plastic plants. The property manager was a middle-aged woman in a fabulous orange and silver-threaded sari that brightened up the lobby. She sat behind bulletproof glass, her eyes glued on a tiny television. Lincoln heard the sound of a Bollywood musical through the glass, orchestral pizzicato arabesques. Taped up behind the woman was a handwritten list of rates and rules. (Rooms could be had by the hour, and for a week.)

He rang the buzzer, and fully expected to be treated like shit. He was, after all, a drifter, and he looked the part. The clothes he had on his back hadn't been washed in a week, and the duffel bag he carried emanated a funky odor. His hands were wrinkled and scarred; they were dishwasher's hands. His nails were bitten to the quick. He hadn't shaved when he took the bus from Ocean City to Shimmer.

The woman behind the glass, however, smiled warmly at him. Even beamed at him. What hair peeked beneath her flame-and-silver veil was black, with a streak of white. Her face was smooth and clear brown.

"Welcome to the Bayside Motel," she said, "and thank you for choosing us!" The speech was boilerplate, but she sold it.

"Thanks," he said. "I'll be needing a room for a couple of weeks. Until I find a permanent place."

"I see," she replied. "Cash or credit?"

"Cash," he said, and handed her a clump of twenty-dollar bills, which would cover a few days.

She made a great production of counting the bills, straightening them, holding them against the light of a lamp, and, finally, marking the bills with a counterfeit-detector pen. Linc was surprised that she didn't smell or taste the money. She placed a magnetic key in the lazy susan cut into the glass display. #28 was handwritten on the key sleeve.

The room was clean, surprisingly so. The teal and orange color scheme was stuck in the early '90s, but the pillows were fluffy, the carpet threadbare but unstained, and the television set was a flat screen. The WiFi password was written on his key sleeve. Best of all, he could see the shimmering marsh from the picture window.

***

Lincoln awoke to the sound of waves, and the bleat of gulls. For a moment, he thought he was back in Ocean City. He'd been there for the summer, drifting from job to job. He'd only had to sleep beneath the boardwalk for a week before he found a room to rent. Frankly, sleeping in the cool sand was preferable to the room he'd rented. The couple that lived down the hall fought constantly, screaming swear words to each other in Czech. Magdalena was also violent. He'd hear slaps and punches, and in the mornings, Lukas would come downstairs with new bruises. Freddie, the man who lived directly beneath him, played old-time gospel music morning, noon and night. Once, Lincoln had gone into his room after he'd left for the day because Mahalia blared from the old boombox Freddie used. Lincoln quickly stepped into the dark room and switched the music off. As he left the room, he stepped over piles—*mountains*—of porn magazines with names like *Jugs* and *Twerking Cum Sluts*.

It had been surprisingly comfortable in the sand. There was a wooden sky above him, and the tarp he used as a bed kept the scuttling sand crabs at bay. The sea sounds, clanging buoys, rolling waves, screeching gulls made falling asleep easy. And there were other perks, too. Lincoln found that the boardwalk after hours was a cruising ground for men on the Down Low. They were mostly white men, and probably 'straight' at home, with wives and kids. The sex was hummingbird-quick. And brutal. Only one guy had kissed him.

The jobs he held were also meaningless, and ephemeral. Two weeks as a cashier at a local supermarket. Night security at a beachfront hotel for the month of June. Dishwasher at a variety of greasy spoons, scraping scrapple and other crud off chipped dishes. Those jobs never lasted long. The Blue Plate Diner's boss had been openly racist, referring to African-American customers as 'Canadians,' as in 'those

Canadians don't know how to tip,' or 'those Canadians are too noisy.' The Mermaid Cafe was staffed by meth-heads, from the tatted-up owner to the waitresses and the clientele. No one ever really ate at the cafe. They just sipped bottomless cups of bad brew. He'd ended up at a pancake house, the kind that had pictures of the various dishes on the plastic menu and full of groups of screaming children.

There was a point when he had been one of those kids, attached to a touristy family. Lincoln's own family might have even visited that very pancake house, and shared a Dutch Baby or two: a crispy soufflé-like jumbo pancake filled with cooked apples, dusted with powdered sugar. Now, he was a nobody, a shadow-dwelling weirdo who lived beneath boardwalks, and rode smelly buses, floating from dead-end job to even deader-end job.

He never imagined this kind of life. He was from a middle-class family, solidly in Huxtable territory. Dad was an epidemiologist, and Mom was a paralegal. His older sister Elaine had gotten into an Ivy League college. They lived in a big house in the Rock Creek Park section of DC, where he saw daily traffic jams and herds of deer. He fully expected to go to college, get a good government job, and have a family. But that all came crashing down when he met Gash.

Garland Ashton was from Southeast, the 'bad' part of the city. He wore jeans that sagged low and showed his underwear riding high and conforming to his shapely buttocks. He listened to Trap music with slurred vocals, minimalist clattering sound effects, and deliberately misspelled words. (Example: all plural nouns had z's instead of s's: words became wordz, cats became catz, etc.) He had a couple of indecipherable tattoos on his forearm, word(z) in ornate script (probably L'il Wayne lyrics) that were olive green against his black skin. Both his parents hated Gash within minutes of meeting him. He could see their frowns of disapproval when Gash refused to take out his earbud while they ate dinner. And Mom threw daggers from her eyes when he took a cellphone call at the table and cussed up a storm.

"Where did you say you met him?" his mother asked after he left the house.

"At Estelle's birthday party," he said.

"Really?"

"Estelle has lots of different friends. Theater kids, math nerds…"

"Hood rats," his father said.

Mom said, "Kenneth!"

"I'm sorry," said Dad, from behind his newspaper shield, "I calls it like I sees it."

Later that night, as Lincoln worked on a history paper, Elaine stood in the door frame. With her long, black hair, delicate features and light skin, she was destined for greatness. (The fact that she was also a Merit Scholar sealed the deal.) Linc wasn't a particularly gifted student, and his odd proportions—too tall, too thin, uneven skin tone—meant that he always felt his imperfections acutely, against his sister's perfection. Her nickname was Elaingel.

The angel Elaine deigned to grace him with her presence, with her Renaissance-frizzy hair.

"I know where you met Gash."

He looked up from his laptop, sighed. "Not you, too."

She glanced down the hall, presumably for their parents. Then she slipped inside his room, closing the door after her.

She leaned against the door, and whispered. "You met him at that gay group that meets on Capitol Hill."

For a second, he thought he misheard her.

Elaingel said, "Stop acting so shocked. I've known you were gay for a while. I think Mom suspects. But she doesn't really care."

Linc did some internal calculations. He'd been very careful. He never brought home gay newspapers, and cleared his browser history every time he looked up gay things (mostly porn).

"You can stop freaking out for a moment or two. I just want you to be careful around Gash. You know that he has a record."

"How do you know that?"

"Carol's sister Jennifer goes to that group. She recognized you."

After a pause, Linc said, "I don't know a Jennifer. Or Jenny."

"She goes by the name 'Jay.'"

Linc immediately saw Jay. She was androgynous, and many of the gay boys in the group initially mistook her for a pretty brown-skinned boy. It was still unclear whether Jay was trans or not. She always wore immaculately black jeans and colorful hoodies that hid her close-shaved hair. He'd met Jennifer years ago, at some party. Then, she'd been real girlie girl, wearing some T-shirt with a glittery unicorn and a hot pink tulle dress.

"I was over at Carol's a couple of weeks ago," Elaine continued. "Jay told us about Gash."

"She gossiped! The group is supposed to be anonymous!"

Elaine waved this issue away, as if it were a gnat. "She was concerned. About you."

"How sweet," he said sarcastically. "I can take care of myself."

"Did you know that he was in juvie?"

"A long time ago."

"Two years is not a long time," Elaine said. "He still does lean. And sells Percocet and oxies."

"How does Jay know this? Did she buy it from him?"

Elaine sighed. "I give up. I'm just saying. Keep your eyes open." She turned and left the room.

He turned back to his paper, but Mary McLeod Bethune's story failed to captivate him. He thought about Gash. The shape of his body, compact and finely etched muscles. The sharpness of his bones, cheek and hips, like knives. The way his skin was purple under certain lights. The thing was, he already knew that Gash was involved in some seedy things. The stint in juvie, the drug-selling rumors were all a part of the legend of Gash.

Linc had met Gash through the youth group, but he'd seen him months before at the main branch of the public library downtown. There was a loosely-knit gang of street kids that hung around the library. They called themselves Violet Rage, and looked to Gash as one of their leaders. Violet Rage was a collection of gay and trans kids of color, a far cry from the mostly white 'official' gay youth group. They hung around the Gallery Place Metro stop when the weather was nice and the MLK Library when it was cold or raining. At the library, they mostly hovered around the free computers, watching videos online.

For months, he surreptitiously spied on Violet Rage, listening in on their conversations, and slowly learned their stories.

There was Simon/Symone, who was cherubically beautiful, with a mane of ringleted hair surrounding their baby-soft face. When they were Simon, they wore ink-black clothes that somehow managed to stay free of lint or dust. Turtlenecks and sweaters, jeans, boots that shone with fresh shoe polish. When they were Symone, the color purple was somehow involved. Symone always wore the same shade of violet eye makeup and lipstick. Linc gathered, from bits and pieces, that they had started the group after some homophobic assault on a metro train. Simon/Symone was beautiful, but they could be vicious. Rumor had it that they had stabbed their attacker with a penknife.

DeMarko was over three hundred pounds and always had one earbud in, whether or not his phone was playing music. His mother was the minister of some storefront church, so he was officially on the Down Low. "She'd exorcize me if she knew. She thinks homosexuality is a demon." Linc laughed aloud when he overheard that. He imagined RuPaul with horns and fangs. He'd quickly moved away from the group that time.

Florette or Flo might have actually been homeless, as far Linc could tell. She always wore the same ratty jeans and carried a backpack that had seen better days. It had rents in the fabric and the color had faded to some godawful blue-gray color. Plus, Flo smelled. Garbage, and unwashed flesh. She would use the free library bathrooms to wash up with that stinging institutional pink soap. She was brash, loud and funny. The library cops were kind of afraid of her. She would start some shit if she thought you were looking at her. "Damn, I know I look good but put your eyes back in their sockets," she said to an ogling security guard.

There were other members of Violet Rage that came and went. It was too loose a gathering to be considered a proper gang, but they all stuck up for each other. He even overheard them talking about 'jumping' bullies at the schools that VR members attended.

Linc thought that he was pretty discreet in scoping the group out. But the Saturday that he first dropped into the LGBTA Youth Group on Capitol Hill, Gash came up to him, and said, "I thought I might see you here."

He stupidly replied, "What do you mean?"

"You thought you was slick, son. But all us Ragers knew that you were eyeing us. But it's cool."

Then Gash smiled, slow and sinister, like a cartoon villain. Linc remembered the dark thrill he felt. It started in his chest, just below his heart, and traveled down his body, ending at his groin. It was like a seed had been planted in him, and it now bloomed. The tendrils snaked through his veins, the leaves unfurling in his bloodstream. He couldn't speak, afraid that he would spit up leaves and petals.

***

Mrs. Doshi gave Linc directions to a coffee shop called Bitter and Sweet that served glazed cake donuts and a strong brew. No fancy lattes or Americanos. The donut was still warm, the sugar glaze still runny. At least that was good. Like the Bayside Motel, the decor was hopelessly stuck in the '80s, with burgundy stools bandaged with duct tape and a peeling Formica countertop. Linc wasn't the only person here. The countertop was taken over by surly-looking watermen in wet wear waders. All of them, both the black and white men, looked ancient. They had the same craggy skin and dour expressions. Linc didn't want his next job to be on a boat, trawling for crabs. Linc hated spiders, and crabs were the sea's version of them. He hated the way they walked, and the weird stalks they had for eyes. He liked being near water. He had no desire to actually *be* on the water.

So far, Shimmer did not impress him. The shore was rocky, and it reeked of dead fish. On the way to the donut shop, which followed the curve of the bay, he saw a dead turtle being attacked by bleating, combative seagulls. The boats that floated out in the water were sludge-colored and flat-bottomed, with no aesthetics. They were just metal boxes. The few people he saw on the street weren't particularly friendly.

But he might not have any choice in picking a job. Funds were getting low. He needed to get a job. Maybe fate would have him adrift on a literal sea.

He scoured an online bulletin board for jobs in Shimmer. There wasn't much available. The few restaurants he saw were at least ten miles out of town and probably required a car. There were no hotels here, just a couple of bed and breakfasts that were closed for the season. Retail was limited to a grocery store—an overnight stocker. Linc hated overnight jobs. He could never get his body to adjust to the hours.

One job, however, did stand out. After he read through the requirements, he made the call without hesitation. (Strike when the iron is hot.)

Five minutes later, he had an interview at the Whitby-Grayson Museum. Linc finished his second donut and wolfed down the scalding coffee.

According to the GPS app on his phone, the museum was a twenty-minute walk away.

5: FUCHSIA

A t first, she saw the girl in flashes. She was a scrawny thing, more like a bundle of sticks than a little girl. She practically swam in her homespun dress. Her features were sharp and birdlike, her eyes took in everything, and found it lacking. At first, she didn't really like the girl. She was a wild thing, tart-tongued and crafty.

Her name, though, was pretty enough. Hazel was a beautiful color, a lovely shade of golden-brown, not unlike the girl's skin tone. And after a while, she began to like Hazel. She loved the way the child moved, quick and determined, and how she was stubborn and high-spirited. She was like a sudden gust of wind, given form.

She still had no name, and no memory. Was she dead, a haint, haunting a place where she lived? Was she an angel, sent to watch over the child? Or was she something else? She decided to put aside the matter of her exact spiritual designation for the time being. She needed a name, a word to place her in time, in space, in context. The gown she wore, that lurid purple-pink mist-like fabric that draped her formless form, must be a clue.

The word floated up like a bubble. The name of the color she wore, which she now took as her own name. It was as beautiful and strange as the color it described.

Fuchsia. Her name, for now at least, would be Fuchsia.

Fuchsia found herself leaving the beautiful marsh, just to watch the child in motion. It didn't bother her that Hazel couldn't see her. Sometimes, she would visit the child every day. Other times, time would have elapsed, and Hazel had grown a bit.

Fuchsia dimly recognized the house Hazel inhabited. The house was three stories made of brick and the entrance was ornate, with a slate porch and pillars. The front grounds were hemmed in by a copse of oak, sumac and sycamore trees. The lawn was well-manicured and a circular garden full of pansies, delphinium, peonies and clematis grew in the shade of a chinaberry tree. Hazel lived with the other servants in a small stone house in the back of the house, which faced the marsh.

When Hazel entered the house, Fuchsia stayed outside, or returned to the beautiful wetlands, with their crystal water and submerged spears of emerald grass. It was as if the house repelled her. Perhaps there was some kind of ward against whatever she was. She could observe Hazel in the slave's quarters that she shared with other the four other servants. She could go into the stable (where Hazel rarely went; she was scared of horses). Fuchsia could even go into the root cellar beneath the house. But the house itself wouldn't let her inside. She could walk around the ivy-covered house. Fuchsia could explore the roof, with its cracked ceiling tiles, where pigeons nested. But the house itself was impenetrable.

When she tried, she would find herself in the marsh, or in a tree, or in the circular garden, beneath the chinaberry tree. Furthermore, time had passed, sometimes an hour, sometimes a week, before she could return. Maybe she wasn't an angel after all. Maybe she was something to be feared.

She came to recognize the faces of the other people who stepped out into the house. The bony-faced lady of the house, the grey-haired patriarch with wild eyebrows. There were two boys, young men, really. The tall, studious red-haired one, the squat, lurching, rough-and-tumble brown-haired one. Both of them were sprinkled with freckles. When they spoke, Fuchsia could understand them, but she immediately forgot what they said. It wasn't important. Their talk was like the cooing of doves, the cawing of ravens, the chirring of crickets.

All of them loved Hazel, even when they chastised her. And Hazel loved them, too. But she seemed to love the land, the shimmering expanse of water and islets just a tad more.

***

One night, Fuchsia visited Hazel. The girl, now fourteen, was ill. An illness, one that made breathing difficult, had touched the house, and the entire Eastern Shore. The boisterous boy had had it for a while. She remembered him sitting on the porch wrapped in a blanket, watching the slaves work.

One day, Fuchsia saw Hazel tremble, then fall like a leaf when she was doing the laundry outside. She waited patiently by the girl's feverish body, listened to the rasp of her breath. If only she could touch the child, or summon help. But Fuchsia was nothing. She was invisible, a will-o'-the-wisp dreamed up by the land, if even that.

So, she waited beside her only friend, who did not even know she existed. She sang to her, even though she did not have voice. She stroked Hazel's sweat-sheened forehead with the drapery of her sleeve. The girl's eyes opened in a squint. They quivered, leaking water.

Hazel said, softly, "I like that dress. It sure is a pretty color." Then her eyes closed again.

***

Judith found Hazel shortly after. She called for Jethro and Caleb to help carry the girl to her bed. Hazel was in a delirium, muttering nonsense about angels, and bright purple robes. "She was the color of the marsh-bell," she told Judith, who lay her in her straw bed.

"Hush, child. You was just seeing things," Judith said. "I remember when the Missus got the fever and was talking to her dead mother."

"But I saw her," Hazel insisted. "She was colored, too. Real dark skinned."

"Jethro, get the brandy and have the Missus get Doctor Walters. Hazel's in a bad way."

Fuchsia watched this exchange silently. *She saw me*, she thought. She burned with excitement. Furthermore, she was in the house. Maybe there was a way to communicate with her. She had been alone for too long. Herons and ospreys were beautiful, but she couldn't talk to them. Then Judith's words—"Hazel's in a bad way"—took on a sinister meaning. Maybe the girl, barely a teenager, was close to death. Fuchsia's aching loneliness wouldn't be cured by Hazel's sudden death. She may not have been an angel, but she didn't wish any harm to come to the girl.

She watched and waited as Judith wiped down Hazel's face with cool rags, when Caleb came with the brandy which he gave to the girl to help her sleep. Fuchsia had no sense of time. Minutes or hours might have passed. She never got tired, and had no need of sleep. She could have gone back to the wetlands and the beauty that she loved. Instead, she stood vigil over the girl. Hazel tossed and turned, her breathing was rapid.

Finally, Doctor Walters arrived. He was a sickly-looking thing himself, bald as a turtle and covered in liver spots. His eyes were pale blue and rimmed in red. He took one look at Hazel, and declared her a consumptive. He didn't even bother to open his medical bag.

"Is there anything you can do to lessen her pain?" Caleb asked. He spoke proper English when he had to.

"She needs to go to a sanitorium," the doctor replied, "but they don't have sanitoriums for niggers. I can give medication for her pain, but she needs a diet of bone broth, plenty of liquids and sleep."

When the doctor left, Judith conferred with Caleb: "I don't think she's long for this world."

"Why do you say that?"

"She said she saw an angel. A *colored* angel."

Caleb said, "You remember how the Missus saw her dead mother when she was sick? I imagine this is the same thing. That colored angel was probably her mother, as she remembered her."

Fuchsia heard this. *Maybe I am the girl's mother.* It was a plausible reason for her connection to the girl. But, somehow, it seemed wrong. She was also joined to the unspoiled land where she lived, that sanctuary where the purple-pink marsh flowers grew. She loved that place the same way she loved Hazel. There was something of the marsh in that girl. Fuchsia couldn't piece it together. This, however, was a mystery to ponder. It was a puzzle, not important. She could figure out the mystery later, when the girl was out of harm's way.

Fuchsia stayed by the girl's bedside for a long time. She was there when the girl was given medicine and broth by the well-meaning but distant Judith. She watched as Jethro and Caleb prayed over her. Even the Missus visited the girl, with a nosegay of lavender pressed to her face. She was also vigilant over the child when no one was around.

She tried touching the sleeping girl, but her hand vanished like smoke upon contact.

Smoke.

Smoke was like breath, vaporous and curling.

It was more like an instinct than an actual idea. Fuchsia bent down, and gently kissed Hazel's lips. They were as soft as petals.

6: XAVIER

"Y ou are welcome to use the laundry," said Iris.

"Bless you," said Xavier. He'd left his umbrella at the museum, and he'd been caught in a sudden downpour. He was dripping wet and his glasses were fogged. He was always losing things, tablets, cellphones, wallets and keys. He'd had to replace credit cards more than once. His mother called him "the Absent-Minded Professor." After he changed upstairs and slipped into sweats, Iris led him down to the basement with a bag of other items that needed washing. Though basement might have been too generous a word. It was more like a cellar. The stairs were steep and creaky. He felt like he was going into a crypt. The stale air didn't help.

Iris turned on the light. It was a single naked bulb and it cast a thin, sickly light on the concrete cave. The cinderblocks were streaked with faded carmine water stains and most of the floorspace was dominated with machines. There were side-by-side washer and dryer units, and what Xavier assumed was a furnace. "It's fairly straightforward. It's an old unit but it still works," Iris said. "I'll be upstairs if you have any questions."

The washer rumbled menacingly after he turned it on. Hopefully it wouldn't eat his clothes, like the laundry room at his dorm sometimes did. His mother had called him earlier that day to check in on him.

"Are you getting enough material for your thesis?" she had asked him.

He had told her yes.

What he hadn't told her was how disappointed he was with the Whitby-Grayson Museum. He had hoped that visiting it and seeing Whitby's and the other artists' work up close would have been, somehow, more meaningful. Xavier was underwhelmed.

He remembered walking to the Whitby-Grayson Museum a couple of days ago. It was a fifteen-minute walk from Iris's place. The houses he passed on the way there were a mixture of weathered wood and putty-colored aluminum siding. Most of them were two stories tall but there were a couple of one-story ramblers that looked like retrofitted double-wide trailers. The few people he saw on the street or getting in cars were African-Americans. Most of the men wore woolen knit caps and rubber waders and boots. The women wore track suits or house dresses. They all had standoffish expressions, neither curious nor welcoming. So much for skinfolk being kinfolk.

When he was a freshman at the college, he'd had vague ambitions to capture uniquely African-American spaces, like this town. Shimmer had a rich history of freedmen who became successful watermen, even when Maryland and Delaware were slave states. Xavier wanted to chronicle this in acrylic, like Jacob Lawrence had painted with gouache and cardboard. Seeing these faces, with their granite expressions, made Xavier want to commit them to canvas. There was something timeless about this place. The trappings of modernity (the cars, the cellular phones) did not hide that this town was isolated, out of time. People still lived by the whims of the bay. Xavier imagined spreading burnt umber and ochre, earth tones and shades of white to capture the bleak scene. He heard the bleating of gulls and saw their black-and-white wings arc over the sleepy town.

Hazel Whitby had walked down these streets. So had Shadrach Grayson. Perhaps they had seen and interacted with some of these folks' ancestors. He could easily see why they would remake the world they knew into something rich and strange. In this wet and grey landscape, Whitby's purple-garbed angel and Grayson's mysterious hovering will-o'-the-wisps gave the bleakness of shore life a touch of mystery.

The work of the Shimmer Artists intrigued him. Their stories implied that there was something else, apart from artistic drive, that made them create. If he was honest with himself, he was fascinated with the idea of 'channeling' creativity. His own work had a dead-on-arrival feel. He'd tried realism and abstraction, watercolor and oils. In the end, his paintings were inert things, waiting for the spark that made Hazel Whitby's work alive. Back at college, there was another black student, Enoch Porter, who claimed that some spirit guide flashed images of what to paint into his brain. At the time, Xavier thought that he was full of shit. Enoch painted pop-art. Warholesque, candy-bright, superficial portraits of Michael Jackson and Prince as messianic figures. It was so obvious. Jackson as many-armed Shiva, Prince as Dionysus in a vineyard. When he was criticized in class for cultural appropriation and the general jejune style, Enoch would say that he had to paint the image in his head, free of self-awareness. The thing was, while Enoch Porter's work was derivative, it popped. You couldn't look away. The vines slithered behind the haloed Prince, Jackson's extra arms were in motion.

Xavier entered what passed for a commercial district in Shimmer, past a restaurant called Bertha's, a boutique and a beauty shop. All three were closed. Shimmer had the feel of a ghost town. Empty, abandoned, echoing with seabird screeches. No cars cruised down the slick streets. Shimmer wasn't a resort town. There were no tourist attractions, just the endless wet marshland. It was the kind of creepy town in horror movies, where the outsider is sacrificed to some ancient ritual.

The museum itself was an ugly industrial building. He'd seen it online many times, but in the harsh grey light, it looked cheap. The online pictures had probably been digitally altered. Xavier felt that Whitby's work ought to be in a more dignified place. He was used to the gravitas of the Smithsonian buildings. Maybe his scholarship would make Whitby's work more well-known.

The museum grounds included a small blocked-in garden. It was wet and there were maybe ten marsh-bells growing out of the soppy soil. What a strange, ugly flower it was. The shape of the flower bells was too long to be aesthetically pleasing. There was something reptilian about the fringes of the petals, and the stamens looked uncomfortably like penises. It didn't help that each flower was made of forty or fifty micro flowers, all with their lolling flaccidity on display. Xavier knew that the marsh-bell was an orchid of some kind, and the word 'orchid' derived from the word for testes. The marsh-bell, however, was just a little too on-the-nose. Looking up at one close up, he could see why the flower had inspired the artists. The color was vibrant. The flowers looked like an obscure percussion instrument.

"They are a bitch to maintain," someone with a deep voice said.

Xavier turned, saw a field of gray coverall fabric. He looked up into the face of the tallest man he had ever seen. He was a few shades darker than Xavier. His skin had blue undertones. His hair was styled in an afro mohawk, stubble around the sides, wooly and unkempt on top. His eyes were light gray, his face smooth.

Xavier was suddenly self-conscious. "Well," he managed to get out, "orchids are notoriously fussy."

"These ones certainly are. They require a special soil, and have to be kept moist constantly," the tall man continued. He was also very thin, almost unhealthily so. There was a gauntness to his cheeks.

Xavier thought that he could probably see his ribs beneath the loosely fitted coverall. His voice was deep, but it had a cadence to it, a softness to the end of his sentences that made Xavier think that he might be queer. Gaydar was mixture of crapshoot guessing and decoding masculinity. There was a feline quality about the way he shaped words. His consonants were gentle caresses, not abrupt stops. People always assumed that Xavier was queer, probably due to his slight stature and delicate features. He didn't mind it that much.

"Is the museum open yet?" Xavier asked him.

"I was just going to unlock it."

"Do you know if Dr. Lenski is in yet?"

"He doesn't come in until noon. Did you have an appointment?"

The custodian let him in the building. It was disappointing. Black tile floors, exposed piping painted a uniform grey, beige walls. There was one main room, dedicated to Hazel's quilts, another one for Shadrach's paintings, and a smaller gallery for people inspired by the two of them. The tapestries were the brightest thing in this drab place. Maybe they were the brightest thing in all of Shimmer.

"I'll let you know when Howard comes in." Xavier glanced back to the tall custodian with the gray eyes. He'd momentarily forgotten him, drinking in the many displayed tapestries.

"I'd appreciate that," he replied. "By the way, I'm Xavier."

"Xavier. Like Professor X?"

"Who?"

"From the X-Men. The comics. The movie with Patrick Stewart. Never mind." He flashed a grin. His teeth were all messed up, yellow tombstones on blackened gums. It was still a nice smile. "I'm Linc, by the way."

Linc left him alone in the museum, probably to attend to those fussy marsh-bells.

Marsh-bells were all over Hazel's work. They bloomed all over the pieces of fabric, like an invasive species. The rest of the tapestries' colors had, somehow, faded. The blues and browns were no longer vibrant, which made the brightness of the magenta shade all the more prominent. When Hazel had made these quilts, magenta dye was relatively rare, reserved for only the wealthiest of families.

The Whitby family was only modestly wealthy, as they were not tobacco farmers like many of their neighbors. So where had Hazel gotten such brilliant fabric?

He had been studying one of the pieces up close when Dr. Lenski came in and introduced himself. Lenski was a fine-featured bald man, slender and in the mold of Dr. Giordano with his retro-spectacles, finely creased shirt and pants. (Lenski also pinged his gaydar. The man was eccentric—he wore clothes only in shades of pink and black. Black outfit, pink tie. A black shirt with pink roses, etc.) He'd given Xavier a tour of the museum and let him use a desk in the tiny office. The archives, while well-maintained, were nowhere near as extensive he expected. The WiFi signal was weak and would drop without warning.

Finally, the artwork seemed, somehow, less, after that first glance at it. It was weird. The works in the archives and in the galleries seemed to be robbed of their unique charm. They were dulled, greyed-out and inert. The Shimmer Artists were known for the way they achieved a kind of primitive trompe l'oeil effect with their use of color that made the work move. Whitby's tapestries could entrance him for hours. Now, they were just lifeless pieces of fabric.

Xavier stewed over his lack of enthusiasm as he did his laundry. Iris helpfully gave him an actual laundry basket. In between the trips to the laundry room, he organized the notes and pictures he had taken. He added the strange palimpsest picture of the marsh-bell in his rented room. Why not? It seemed to have more vigor than the work he'd seen at the gallery.

Something caught his eye when he went down to the laundry

room. Opposite the machinery were clear plastic storage tubs, neatly stacked up. The bin on the bottom was marked in masking tape with the name Tamar Dupré.

Xavier recalled that Dupré was one of the names of the Shimmer Artists in the collection.

"Well, shit," he mumbled.

"Is everything okay?" Iris's voice came from upstairs.

"Everything's… my clothes aren't dry yet. That's all."

"It takes a couple of times to get really dry. I've been meaning to have that dryer looked at. Just start it again."

"Thanks," he said. He was glad that she didn't come down to check on him. He started the dryer again and it rattled.

The top bin wasn't heavy. It was just large, unwieldy and tightly tucked into its alcove. It took some jimmying to move the huge gray box out of its cubby. Whatever sounds he made were masked by the machine's sound. He thought he heard Iris retreat from the kitchen, but he worked quickly just the same. With the storage bins taking up most of the space, Xavier felt slightly claustrophobic, which added to his slight paranoia. The palette of gray on gray, the bleeding walls, the lone lightbulb… The underground room felt forgotten, neglected.

He peeled off the top of the bin and found that it was filled with many pieces of cardboard. By the dim light, Xavier saw the floral motif, and the glitter of lustrous purple. It was similar to the picture that hung above his bed, that same layered collage style of tissue paper and obscured images. He saw black women's faces hiding behind or in the center of flowers. The images had been cut out from magazines or fabric and wallpaper samples. Then she had used a clear drying glue to meld the juxtapositions together.

Iris must have known Tamar. How else would she have gotten this motherlode of work?

***

He found the book four years after the first time he saw the quilt Edyie Baird owned. He was fifteen at the time, and he had vague interests in being an architect. Drawing was the only thing he was passionate about. Everything else bored him to tears, even though he was a good student. There was something about the smell of pencil lead, and calling something into existence, be it a trigonometry figure or the more complicated shapes he eventually created. His class notes were always filled with doodles. At first, geometric shapes, mathematically precise triangles and three-dimensional cubes. Then he began drawing figures. Bird-headed men, sphinxes, and things from mythology.

At some point, Xavier knew that this was not just an idle hobby. It was the core of who he was. He experimented with graphite, chalk, and ink. He moved into strict realism. Portraits of fruit, quick sketches of people on the metro, buildings on the National Mall, copies of things in the Smithsonian.

For his fifteenth birthday, he got an iPad, along with an electronic stylus. That's when Xavier started posting his work on Deviant Art under the name Xemplar. (The logo was in a heavy serif font, all caps, with X purple, his tribute to Prince.) He developed a fan base. At one point, he had nearly 800 followers. He even got a commission here and there. (Mostly drawings of pets or RPG characters.)

Xavier started scouring eBay and used bookstores for art books. He could draw, but he felt hopelessly ignorant. He amassed a decent library of slightly worn coffee table-sized art books and smaller Time/Life Edition survey books on Impressionism, Surrealism and Romanticism. He skimmed the texts, opting instead to copy the paintings in the books. He absorbed everything through visual and muscle memory. Shading, light, color theory were all acquired by obsessive practice.

Then he found *Strange Gardens: The Quilts of Hazel Whitby* in a remainder bin. The book was in good condition. Even the dustjacket was intact. Before Xavier bought the book, he flipped through it. The tapestries, reproduced in full color, were as vivid as ever. And the spots of magenta in the abstract maps still shimmered, as if they were animated blobs. The book was only ten dollars, significantly discounted from the $39.95 list price. He saw the black stripe on the deckled edge that marked it as a remainder. There was only one copy of the art book. Most remaindered books came in sets.

When he bought the book, he could have sworn the cashier said, "Huh," in a slightly derisive manner as she searched for the bar code. He thought nothing of it.

He started reading the book on the bus ride back home. Reading, not just looking at the pictures. Xavier knew that if he looked at those photos of Whitby's quilts, he would become hypnotized by the motion of the tapestries, and trapped in the threads.

The book had a scant history about Whitby:

Hazel Whitby was sent as a gift from Mrs. Whitby's sister Laura Osborn, shipped up from South Carolina with two barrels of rice and several lengths of Corsican lace. The child began creating her odd floral quilts shortly thereafter, perhaps inspired by the change of scenery.

He flipped through the introduction, trying to find an explanation for the technique she used for the fluttering color effect. The author mentioned it in the last paragraph.

Hazel Whitby's tapestries have a shimmering quality, created by a subtle and sophisticated use of minute clashing colors. The precision of her stitch work is a marvel of trompe l'oeil artistry. Whitby's muse was the Eastern Shore where she lived. She imbued her work with an almost Blakean mysticism…

***

A strange garden spread out before Xavier on the cold concrete floor of the cellar. A wetland scene, under the watchful eyes of a giant marsh-bell. Dupré had used photographs, cutouts from magazines and catalogs and greeting cards, construction and tissue paper to create variations on the same landscape. These images and materials were mostly layered upon stock board, but there were some plates, and old Reader's Digest books covered with images.

Xavier wanted to drag the whole bin up to his room, and catalog them. He didn't think that Iris would approve. Instead, he laid out each piece on the concrete floor, and took a picture of them with his phone. By the time he was done, it was almost eleven o'clock.

He carefully placed the artwork back in the bin, and put it back. He thought about how poorly they were kept, in the dank cave of a basement. *Finally, a discovery! But how will I talk to Iris about it? She keeps them for herself, for some reason…*

He couldn't figure out why.

7: LINCOLN

Since he grew up in the District of Columbia, Linc was used to museums being free, beautifully designed temples to art and learning. In his past, before his current nomadic life style, he had been to many museums, both in his own city and others. The Louvre, the Tate Modern, the Chicago Museum of Art. Museums were sterile, well-lighted, and full of wide-open spaces. They were architectural marvels, like the brutalist concrete circle that was the Smithsonian's Hirschhorn, or they were repurposed palaces. The Whitby-Grayson Museum, however, was the opposite of those.

It looked like an old processing plant of some kind. It was a single-story low building, with baby blue-colored aluminum siding and a metal roof that was ridged like a ruffled potato chip. Since it was right on the water, Linc could imagine it being a fish processing plant. Watermen could have brought the day's catch to this building, where one hundred or so workers chopped and portioned bluefish, bass, or picked crabs for lump meat. The whole place probably once stank of fish guts and the parking lot was lined with pinkish, bloody water. It was an ugly building, a rude eyesore on the landscape.

At least the entrance was nice. The name of the museum was spelled out in metal letters, in industrial tones of copper, nickel-gray and some iridescent-looking metal that had peacock colors rippling across it. Linc tried the door. It was locked. There was a doorbell with the unmistakable black circle of a tiny camera housed in a lozenge of plastic. He pressed this, self-conscious of the length of his hair and the dinginess of his clothes. The contraption lit up, the red dot of the camera active and focused on him. That little red light stayed on for what seemed like a long time before he was buzzed in.

He walked into a brightly lit lobby, buzzing with fluorescent tubes that were reflected in the sleek sealed concrete floor. A middle-aged white man sat behind an information desk. He had buzzed his hair, but it was just growing in. Linc could see patches of gray and reddish-brown worming their way up from the pink scalp, a pattern replicated in his goatee. He was thinnish, save for an incongruous lumpy stomach that appeared out of nowhere, out of context. He wore a pink gingham shirt that looked as if it had been ironed within an inch of its life. And his glasses frames were hot pink. He was maybe a foot shorter than Linc was.

"We don't open until eleven," the man said. His voice was high and slightly effeminate, with the faint hint of a Baltimore accent. He sounded gay. Linc seized on to those facts. He knew he looked unprofessional and rumpled. He hadn't had a chance to do laundry, so he was aware of the musty odors wafting from his shirt. (At least he had changed his undergarments.) He was aware that he was a tall black man who exuded an aura of homelessness.

"I am here because of the job ad," Lincoln said. He made sure to articulate each word.

"Ah," said the man. "Yes, that. I've never had anyone just walk in like that." He looked ill-at-ease.

Linc gave him his best smile. He knew that some of his teeth were discolored, and that there was some facial wasting evident. But he also knew that he could be charming when he wanted to be.

"Well, I've never just walked in for a job before. Here's to firsts." (This last statement was a boldfaced lie. Most of the jobs he applied for as he drifted about the Eastern Shore were responses to HELP WANTED signs.)

"Do you have a résumé?" The man with the hot pink glasses stepped out from behind the information desk. He also wore hot pink socks.

"No, I do not," he said. "I just got into town. My name is Lincoln White. I am a dependable worker…"

"I'm sure you are, Lincoln."

"Call me Linc. For short." Lincoln extended his hand, and kept eye contact with the man. That's when he noticed the guy's eyes. They were the oddest shade of green that he had ever seen. They were almost yellow, the color of key limes. They clashed with his aggressively pink outfit.

"All right. Linc. I'm Howard. Howard Lenski." He clasped the offered hand. Linc knew that he had large hands. His hand engulfed the delicate hand of Howard. Howard's hand was soft and dry, like paper. His own hands were rough and callused. At least his nails were cut, so there were no crescent moons of dirt beneath them.

"Howard," Linc said, slowly letting go of his hand, "I am a hard worker. I've done custodial work many, many times. I am happy to send you references." (He was pretty sure that Jessi at the Lighthouse Hotel would give him a good recommendation.)

"I have a couple of interviews lined up," Howard said. Linc could tell he was lying because Lenski broke eye contact, and besides, Linc was a seasoned liar himself.

"I'm willing to do anything. Anything. Nothing is beneath me."

He saw the calculations going on in Howard Lenski's mind. This was a risky gambit. He hoped that he hadn't come on too strongly. But he was desperate. He needed the money. Linc would be out on the streets in a week, and it was no longer summer. He could imagine the wet, damp cold sneaking into his clothes, into his bones. A podunk art gallery was more appealing to him than dock work.

"I," Howard stammered and stalled. *He's a closet case,* Linc thought, *and he's unsure if I'm flirting with him.* If it came to it, he might give Lenski a hand job. He'd certainly done worse. Middle-aged white guy was something of a staple beneath the boardwalks. "Well, Mr. White. Lincoln. Linc. I'm in a bit of a jam. A pickle. The last custodian here left on bad terms. Suddenly."

Linc nodded in sympathy. "I grew up around museums. I'm a DC native. The Smithsonian was my playground."

"I'm from Baltimore, myself." *Good. I'm in,* thought Linc. "The Whitby-Grayson Museum is hardly in the same league as the Smithsonian. As you can see." Howard Lenski waved his arm, indi-cating the off-white walls, the flickering light tubes. The museum was bare bones.

Howard continued speaking, but the words fell to the back-ground. One of the hanging frames had caught Linc's eye. What drew him to the wall was the psychedelic wash of color. He'd done a little research about the Whitby-Grayson Museum. Read a Wiki-pedia article about the quilts and the paintings. The images in the wiki did not do justice to the work. The colors were so vibrant, so bright that they seemed to move. The green and the blue and the brown cloth were slightly worn. But the bright pink-purple blooms practically pulsed.

He thought he was hallucinating. Linc was reminded of three-dimensional postcards, the ones made of heavy card stock, that changed every time you moved them. Jesus or the Virgin, their eyes closed one way, opened another. Those wild, impressionistic smears of color, not the pink of Valentines, nor the purple of Prince in his regalia, but somehow, both, and neither.

"Are you familiar with Hazel Whitby's work?" Howard inter-rupted him.

"A little," he said, absently. His eyes moved across the abstract fabric, trying to make sense of it. "It's amazing."

He moved to another tapestry. This one was just flares of magenta, with lightning strikes of dark blue. The third quilt was circular, bright blue in color, and in the center, a single spot of that peculiar hue. It drew Linc's eye in until he felt that he was swimming in some lagoon. He moved toward the flickering flame through the shallow water.

Lenski's voice pulled him back from the lagoon, brought him back on land. He reluctantly turned toward the man, knowing that he no longer wanted to work here. He *needed* to work here. Suddenly, the museums of the Smithsonian seemed like airless mausoleums. This museum, however, seemed alive.

"You know, Gerald, the last custodian, the one who quit, couldn't stand the artwork. He told me, 'It's too loud.' He also thought the museum was haunted."

"It's brilliant," Linc said, and really meant it. "I mean, it's like Rothko. Like Sam Gilliam." The references came tumbling out of his mouth of their own accord. He wasn't trying impress Lenski with his bougie background. But there are some things that, when you first see them, they seem perfect. Things that can break you, things that call to you. Things that make you see your true self.

These strange quilts, with their odd geometric and bold colors, made Lincoln White feel human. And he hadn't felt human in a long, long time. He'd been a walking scarecrow, haunting the Eastern Shore where he'd spent many a vacation with his family. The family that now didn't speak to him, that had cast him out like a rag.

Lenski said, "Hazel has that effect on some people. And to others, her work just looks like a mess."

"It *is* a mess," Linc said. "A beautiful mess."

Whatever wariness Howard Lenski felt melted away. Linc could see it fall away from his face. The man's whole body relaxed. "When can you start?" he asked.

8: IRIS (1979)

Thirteen was a summer of ghosts.

Gilead Baptist was just around the corner from Pop-Pop's house, and since her grandfather was a religious man, there was no avoiding services. It was summertime, and she was thirteen, and chafing under Pop-Pop's rules. By this time, Aunt Earline had moved out of the house in to her own apartment, so it was back to the three of them. Mom and her aunt didn't get along. They were always fussing at one another. Iris still missed seeing Aunt Earline every day. She always stuck up for her. And she did not believe in the religious indoctrination of children. "Let them come to God on their own time, on their own terms," she said. Aunt Earline would let her stay home on Sundays.

That was over now. Now she was back in itchy, stiff church clothes. Mom still insisted on her wearing ribbons in her hair, as if she were a little girl. The dress she wore looked like a nightgown, a peach tunic with a lace ruffled collar. She had black patent leather shoes and white stockings. She looked like a little old lady. The other girls wore more modern clothes. Some of them even wore dress pants with nice blouses.

Sunday School was held in the church basement, before services began. The ground-level windows, cinderblocks painted bright yellow and the grimy tile made the place look like a prison. Her fellow inmates slowly shuffled in. Many of them went to school with her, and like in school, they hung together in cliques. The cohort was a mix of ages, from five-year-olds to younger teens. Because Iris was not popular, she sat with the younger kids. Since she was dressed like a little girl, she might as well sit with the little kids. *I look like Shirley Temple*, she thought.

The desk seats were arranged in a semi-circular pattern, facing the blackboard. A picture of a haloed Jesus, with long blondish-brown hair and holding a lamb, was taped on the left wall. To the right of the blackboard were discarded felt banners. Iris sat in the second to last seat, next to the banners, a fellow outcast.

Miss Beryl was the Sunday School teacher. She was a plump, pretty woman who wore flowered dresses and seemed to change her wigs often. Today's wig was curly black hair, with reddish high-lights. Some of the kids called her Miss Barrel due to her weight.

She walked into the classroom, taking her place at the black-board.

"Good morning, and God bless you," she positively sang. "Now let us bow our heads in prayer."

During the Lord's Prayer, Iris felt someone come into the room. They took the empty seat next to her. Iris glanced at the new person when the prayer was over.

She gasped.

"Iris?" asked Miss Beryl.

"It's just… Nothing."

Someone snickered. Iris knew that people thought she was weird. That some people referred to her as Ritz, like the crackers. As in, Rissy is crackers. Ritz the Ditz. It used to bother her. Now, she could hardly blame them. For the most part, she kept the things she saw under wraps. She tried not to react when she saw the haloes of color radiating from people. Most people's auras were transpar-ent things that could be ignored, but occasionally there would be someone whose colors demanded attention. Their haloes would warp and tremble, stretch and contract. It was nearly impossible not react to it. They were like silent fireworks. One of her teachers complained that Iris was a good student, but had focus problems. She told no one about this ability. It might have gotten back to Pop-Pop, and who knows what he would have done? Maybe he would banish her, like he did to Aunt Earline.

What she saw sitting next to her, in church of all places, was not a person. It was the shape a girl of about six or so. But it had no features, no hands, or legs. Just the silhouette. The girl-shape was made of an undulating, ever-changing calico-print fabric. Tiny multicolored starburst flowers in tones of pink, blue and red rippled where she would have had a face, or hair. Every now and then, an eye, or a mouth would blur into existence before it unraveled away.

Iris couldn't pay attention to Miss Beryl's lesson about the Good Samaritan. She tried her best to ignore the most intrusive vision yet. When the class was over, Miss Beryl marched the class upstairs to worship with their families. Iris was the last to leave before Miss Beryl turned the lights off. She still saw the Calico Girl, sitting patiently in the seat.

***

The neighborhood where Iris lived was full of abandoned row houses. They were like rotten teeth. Every third or fourth house was boarded up or had broken windows. The front yards were full of weeds and the stairs had moss growing in the cracks. She had to pass these houses every day to get to the store, to school, or to the library.

About a week later, her mother sent Iris out to pick up some groceries at Sonya's Market, a corner store a block away. Iris loved going to Sonya's because they had a store cat, a friendly orange tabby named Comet. On her way back home, she passed by the once mint green abandoned house in the middle of the same block as Sonya's. There was a person standing in the front yard. The shape of a man, with an Afro. He was golden, the color of ginkgo tree leaves in bloom. That bright, painful gold that almost seared the retina. The Gingko Man walked around the front yard, a pitiful crop of dirt, broken glass and struggling clover, then turned toward the house.

He walked through the boarded-up door with its bright orange Caution sticker. It was a conflagration of color.

It's not real, Iris told herself. *He's not real.* She walked past him.

***

The Calico Girl wasn't present the following Sunday, or the next one. It was a shock to see her return almost a month later, in the middle of the repast after services.

The repast was the best part of going to church. Women bought a variety of food to the basement hall. It was served buffet-style, along with cold drinks and punch for the children. Iris loaded up her paper plate with smothered chicken, three bean salad, a couple of rolls and macaroni and cheese. She eyed the dessert table, with its array of cakes and cookies, deciding then and there to at the very least get a slice of Mrs. Wilkins' coconut cake. She sat down at a random kids' table. Two of her classmates from Glaser Junior High, Dionne Franklin and Eunice Bissonette, were also seated at the table. Their Sunday Best was fashionable, dresses in solid colors accented by low high heels. Dionne had her ears pierced, and Eunice wore lip gloss. Iris felt frumpy next to them. Her mother would never let her get away with those outfits.

"Hello, Iris," said Eunice. "You're looking nice."

Iris tried to read the expression on the girl's face. *Is she being nice or sarcastic?* She gave up. She couldn't read faces. But she could see auras, and tonal shifts and vibrations usually meant something. Both of them radiated a cherry-red color that was stable.

"Thank you," Iris said, and smiled. "I like your lip gloss. And I love your earrings, Dionne."

"These things?" said Dionne. "They're just starters."

"I like the color. They're cute."

The three of them chatted, small talk about other classmates and teachers, their summer plans. The conversation flowed naturally, and Iris felt a buoyancy in her chest. It was a bubble that floated up to her brain like a helium balloon.

Then she saw the Calico Girl, out of the corner of her eye, a flash of floral motion. She—it—moved through the crowd, weaving between legs and tables. Every now and then, when she had to, the Calico Girl would move through solid objects. When she did so, something happened. A table shuddered, a chair tipped a little, a person zoned out or reflexively scratched something. It was fascinating, really. Better than cartoons. It was also—sinister.

"You should come up some time," Eunice said.

Iris snapped back to the conversation. Eunice had been talking about her family's summer place in Cape May.

"I mean, it's just a condo," Eunice continued. "But they let us, that is, my brother and me, have guests for a weekend or so."

"That would be nice," Iris said.

The Calico Girl had wandered into the kitchen. Maybe she would stay there.

Dionne said, "Cape May is nice for that Ye Olde Fashioned stuff. I like where my folks go: to Atlantic City. All of those fabulous hotels. You ever been?"

"Yes. Once." She remembered Atlantic City being both seedy and gaudy at once. The whole neon mega-hotels fronted a slum no better than the one she grew up in. The people on the crowded boardwalk all had the same hollowed out look, black or white, male or female. The casinos just sucked their souls dry. The sound of slot machines, the tacky decor, the crush of crowds made her feel dizzy.

"I can't wait to get back up there," Dionne said.

"There's too much white trash up there," Eunice replied. "They look all greasy."

"As if there aren't PWT up in Cape May. Cape May is a bargain basement Martha's Vineyard."

Iris couldn't tell whether they were fighting for real or not. Their cherry-red auras didn't flicker, not once. She was about to say something, maybe about her own paltry family summer plans when the ghost, or whatever it was, stepped out of the kitchen and continued its invisible rampage of small disturbances. It passed through Pop-Pop's wheelchair. One wheel spoke moved forward, straining against the brake. It passed through the dessert table. A tiny shower of crumbs fell on the black-and-green linoleum. No one noticed. No one, except Ritz the Ditz.

"What are you looking at?" Eunice said, her voice startling Iris.

"Nothing," she said, peeling her eyes from the Calico Girl's antics. She thought, *Is she looking for someone? Does she even see the living people around her?*

Dionne peered in the direction of the dessert table. "She was looking at that coconut cake."

She silently thanked Dionne for changing the subject.

***

Walking into Aunt Earline's apartment was like walking into another world. Earline had rented an efficiency in Center City, a primarily white neighborhood. Most of the buildings there were prim and proper colonials and row houses. There was history beneath the brick sidewalks and cobblestone streets. Every other building had some official plaque. Ben Franklin walked here! George Washington stayed over there! It was also a bustling business district, full of trendy boutiques and restaurants. It had taken Iris an hour to get to the building, both by bus and rickety SEPTA train ride. There was a gingko tree in front of the building. She remembered the eerie golden man she'd seen in her own neighborhood with a shudder.

Earline lived on the fifth floor of the building. Her apartment was tiny, but it was stuffed full of amazing things. The walls, for instance, were hung with wooden masks. Masks with horns and tusks. Masks that looked like animals and masks that looked like people's faces. In another context, some of the faces would be scary. But the context was Aunt Earline, so these scowling, placid or angry wooden faces were oddly comforting. The window sills were full of potted plants, things in terra-cotta with trailing or coiling leaves.

She was on the phone when the door opened. "Calm down, sis. She's right here. I just buzzed her in." Earline rolled her eyes at Iris.

"Hi, Mom," Iris said loudly as she took in the weird splendor of Earline's tiny apartment.

"She wants to talk to you." Earline handed her the receiver.

"You promise to be on your best behavior?" her mother asked her.

"Yes. I'm not three."

"Don't give me any attitude, girl. I love you."

"I love you, too."

When she hung up the phone, Earline said, "She's overprotective. But only because she loves you."

"I guess so," Iris replied. Though she disagreed. Mona Broome was overprotective because she was a control-freak. Earlier that summer, Iris stopped wearing ribbons and child-like barrettes in her hair. Her mother actually argued with her over something that insignificant. Pop-Pop stopped the fight. "Let the child wear her hair the way she wants to. Stop fussing over her!"

They spent the weekend together. It was a nice change from being in the house. Pop-Pop didn't believe in air-conditioning the second and third floors of his house during the day, so all of them were cramped in the front room during the August heat. That meant hours of watching Billy Graham on the television, and her mother fussing over Pop-Pop. The drone of the big window unit and the slow stir of the ceiling fan were their only weapons against the wall of humidity that awaited them in the other areas of the house. Earline's efficiency was nicely cool.

Earline's shelves were lined with books. Iris had never seen so many books outside of a library. A couple of them lay open on Earline's bed. There was a tiny desk by the window, which overlooked a parking lot. On the desk, there was a typewriter and a legal pad filled with Earline's spidery handwriting. Was she writing a book? Iris was in love with this tiny apartment, every square inch of it. However, there was one thing missing.

"Where's the TV?" Iris said.

"I don't have one," said Earline. "Do you want something to drink?"

"Sure. A Pepsi would be nice."

"I don't have Pepsi. I have water and orange juice."

When Earline lived with them, she never watched television. Not even the news. She would retire to her room upstairs while the rest of the family watched programs. Iris recalled her calling TV "The Idiot Box" and claiming that it dulled people's intelligence. *Of course, she wouldn't have a television*, Iris thought. She wasn't so sure that she could live exactly the way Earline did.

The glass of juice was strangely bitter and full of pulp.

Black Gnosis had been a back-to-nature group, at least according to her mother. They worshipped a black goddess and believed all sorts of heathen nonsense. When she spoke to Earline about her days with Black Gnosis, her aunt made it seem like just a denomination of Christianity, another flavor like Lutheranism or Seventh Day Adventist. They didn't *worship* Sophia, the Black Madonna of Wisdom. They just honored her as a part of the Godhead. "God has a feminine aspect," were the words she used. It sounded pretty out-there, to be honest. Her grandfather thought Black Gnosis was one of those "wacky, made-up religions," like the Moonies. They had blasphemous ideas, and he was overjoyed when Earline left them. Iris thought she still held onto some of their beliefs. No TV, and unsweetened orange juice seemed to be a little bit hippyish. Along with her unprocessed hair and the fact that Earline wore no makeup.

Iris had been looking forward to this weekend. But she couldn't conceive of what they would do without a television. Television was more than just the programs. It was an organizing principle, something to spur conversation. It was an engine, a driver of social behavior. She could tell time via the programming, and the chatter and laugh tracks gave structure to her day. What else was there to do? Shadow puppets? She had hoped to see one of the movies that were banned in her house. *The Exorcist* was coming on this evening. Watching a scary movie with Earline would have been fun.

She shouldn't have worried. Earline took her shopping on Market Street. Market Street was full of stores that sold things like crystals, jewelry and incense, things Iris didn't even know existed. There was a store that sold the African print fabrics Earline loved, and another store that just sold maps, the antique kind with sea monsters in the margins. There were tobacco stores and tattoo shops. Tons of restaurants, from pizza joints to fine dining. The street was full of the kind of people Iris never saw in her neighborhood. White people with impossibly colored hair arranged in spikes or mohawks. People of all colors who wore ripped clothing, or studs on their jeans, or T-shirts that had dirty sayings. She tried not to gawp at them. It was hard not to.

She trailed along with Earline, who seemed to know a couple of the shopkeepers, as she bought various things, like earrings or a pick for her hair. Earline took her to a record shop, its bins full of albums with weird artwork and then to a used bookstore whose shelves were haphazardly stuffed with paperbacks. Earline left her to explore the store. Iris found herself in the Erotica section, where she pored over books titled *The Sex God of Redondo Beach* or *Wicked Lesbians*. There were some books that even had pictures of men and women naked. Looking at the images of sex organs was simultaneously thrilling and nauseating. She left the Erotica aisle when she heard Earline calling her name.

By the time they had finished shopping, they had walked the entire length of the street. There still were places Iris wanted to visit.

"I know it's a few hours off, but have you thought about what you wanted to eat for dinner?" Earline asked her.

"Anywhere on this street!" she said.

Earline laughed. "Your mama keeps you locked up like a caged bird."

"I know. I hate it. I had to argue to let me wear jeans and a T-shirt. She dresses me up like a baby doll."

"Oh, that Mona. If you had known her when she was your age…."

"How was she when she was younger?" Iris asked. The late afternoon crowd was full of ambling couples, holding hands or hugging.

"You have got to promise to keep this secret. Just between you and me. Swear?"

"I swear!"

"Before she met your father, Mona was a bit of a wild child. She smoked cigarettes when she was your age. I remember the horse whipping Daddy gave her when he found out. She was suspended at least three times during junior high. Once for playing dice! She put Mama and Daddy through hell."

"Really?" Iris said.

Iris couldn't believe her ears. Her straight-laced, uptight mother as a juvenile delinquent was impossible to imagine. Her mother, who wouldn't let her listen to the radio because of all the racy lyrics. Her mother, who told her that babies came from the stork up to and including age eleven. Iris thought of the teenage tough girls she'd seen in *Grease*. Her mother was a reverse Sandra Dee: she went from tight leather and garish makeup to dowdy dresses with lace trim.

"Yes," Earline replied. "She got herself under control by the time she left high school. She had a 'Come to Jesus' moment. But you didn't hear it from me!"

***

They had dinner at Esme's, a French restaurant just off Market Street. It was a small room with a bar, and drenched in atmosphere. The restaurants Iris was used to had pictures of the food on the menus. Esme's was candlelit, the flickering flames barely illuminating a room of ancient wooden floors, white table cloths, and booths girded with purple damask curtains. Oval portraits of women in elaborate hats stared at them from the walls. The servers wore crisply ironed outfits, white shirts with bow ties (even the women) and black slacks.

The bread was crusty and warm from the oven. The French onion soup was rich, and the steak and fries she ordered was tender, the shoestring potatoes crunchy and perfectly salted. For dessert, she and Earline shared a chocolate eclair.

Iris sat back and watched the interesting array of fellow diners while Earline drank a cappuccino. This was the life she should have

had. The life that she deserved. She felt like a grown-up. Sophisticated, like a movie star. She was the only kid in a room full of
adults discussing important things over food that was both delicious and beautiful. Each dish, from the salad placed in front of
one woman to the dessert placed in front of a young man, was a
work of art. The wine glasses were filled with exotic liquids, mostly
in tones of purple and pink. The candlelight cast slowly changing
shadows against whitewashed walls.

The drowsy, warm seed of euphoria bloomed in her chest. It was
a flame-flower roughly where her heart would be.

Then, her happiness ended, right then and there. She became
Ritz the Ditz once again.

One of those *things* entered the restaurant, a woman-shaped slice
of darkness. This silhouette was in an A-frame dress, and she was
short, not much taller than Iris. The fullness of her bosom and her
wide hips were the only things that let her know she was a grown
woman. She was the most nightmarish apparition Iris had seen yet.
It was not in the way she paced about the room. It was in her color.
Her darkness. This was no ordinary black. It was too dark, too tex-
tured. It wasn't the black of a starless night. It was jet. And the jet
of her substance wasn't solid. It moved, like a rustle of fabric or the
heavy fall of oil in water.

"Iris, are you all right?"

She pulled her eyes away from the mesmerizing figure, and
looked at her aunt. A furrowed expression of concern was on her
face, wrinkle patterns on her forehead, a glint in her eye. Her gold-
en halo had a touch of green at the edges, feathered wisps.

"I…" she started.

"You don't look well," Earline said as she touched Iris's forearm.

"I'm good," she said, unconvincingly.

"You sure?"

The woman of moving darkness went into the kitchen.

"Yes," she replied.

But she wasn't fine. Far from it.

***

"Aunt Earline?"

They had just gone to bed. A few minutes had passed, and Iris's vision adapted to the grain of the darkness. (Though, it wasn't truly dark. Light from the street leaked in through the window.)

"Yes?" Earline said. Iris saw her shape in the bed, the shimmer of her golden translucent outline.

"Can I tell you a secret?"

"Of course." Iris heard the note of concern, and felt the tears building up behind her eyes. One of them escaped, streaking her left cheek.

"I think I'm going crazy," she said. And she told Earline about the Calico Girl, the Gingko Man, and the appearance of the Jet-Black Woman. She told her about the halos she sometimes saw around people, and how they could flare or fade, depending on people's moods. At some point, Earline turned on the light and just quietly listened. When Iris was finished, they sat in silence for a while.

"Thank you for trusting me with your story," Earline finally said. "I'm glad you told me."

"So, you think I'm going insane?" Iris couldn't look at her aunt. She was afraid of what she might see in her face.

Earline laughed. More of a snort than a laugh, but still. "I don't think you're crazy at all. Lots of people have visions. Or callings. It's no different than when people at church get the Spirit. I think the things that you see are messages of some kind."

"Messages? From who?"

"Have you heard of Joan of Arc, Iris? No?" Earline got up and began rummaging through her bookshelves. She brought out an oversize book with glossy coated pages. A couple of moments of furious flipping through the book ensued before she found the right page. She placed the opened book in front of her. Iris looked at the picture of a sharp-featured white girl armed with a sword. Behind her was a flowering tree and three ghostly figures with haloes—one woman, two men. "She was a French peasant girl in the 14th century who led an army. She started having visions of angels when she was around your age. She described them as lights."

"What happened to her?"

"Well, it's complicated," said Earline. "She was allowed to lead an army, on the strength of her visions. But she also was a victim of a backlash, and was denounced as a heretic. The point is, she was a visionary. She saw things that ordinary people didn't see. And she was misunderstood, but ultimately granted sainthood for her abilities."

"So, they thought this Joan chick was crazy?" (Ritz the Ditz. She didn't tell Earline about that; it was too embarrassing.)

"Some people did. Others didn't. They saw her as gifted. Even, blessed."

"When she was denounced, what did they do to her? Did they hang her, like those witches in Salem?"

"Iris," Earline said, "you're missing the point. You can choose to view your visions as a curse. But you can also see them as a kind of gift."

The colored haloes of living people, the shimmering dead were all messages of some kind? So far, Iris could just see those things. They did not interact with her. They weren't necessarily frightening. In fact, the colors and textures were quite beautiful, which made them even more disturbing. If the ghosts moaned or were hideous, at least she would know what to do. These luminous shapes that randomly appeared had no apparent meaning or motive.

"I think I know what you're saying," Iris said. "It might be a blessing. But I definitely shouldn't tell Mother or Pop-Pop. They'd think it was a curse."

"Oh, by no means tell those two," Earline said. "They certainly wouldn't get it."

Not too longer after, Earline switched the light off. Fire-red blobs of color slowly faded behind Iris's closed eyelids.

Joan of Arc wasn't hung, she thought as she drifted off, *she was burned at the stake.*

9: FUCHSIA (1840)

Hazel's mind was quick as a water moccasin coiling through the swamp. As quick as a hare bounding through the brush, as quick as the fox that chased the hare. Quick as a heron diving for a fish, as quick as the fish slipping through the talons. Thoughts went here—and there—and here again. Her moods changed colors, like the seasons. From placid green spring happiness to fiery red autumn leaf angry. Winter cool sadness, summer bright manic joy.

For a good while, Fuchsia floated like a leaf on the hurricane of Hazel's thoughts. She found no mooring, nothing she could hold on to. She was buffeted and overwhelmed with the cascade of emotion and word, image and touch and smell. The child buzzed and burned with demonic energy, flitting from situation to stimuli.

I hate laundry day. They ought to clean their own shit-stained small clothes! Why does Missus always be rebuking me? Master drinks too much. I wonder what tobacco smoking is like? I wish I could wear some fine clothes every once and a while. I swear they have a raccoon in the attic; I can hear it scritch-scratching away!

Her thoughts were an endless, relentless rush that drowned Fuchsia. There was no rhythm. Entering the girl had seemed like such a good idea at the time. Now she regretted it.

Almost regretted it.

There were things that kept Fuchsia in Hazel's body. While she couldn't smell, or taste or touch anything, she felt the deep emotions Hazel felt when her senses were engaged. She might not know what Judith's biscuits tasted like slathered with butter and honey, but pleasure exploded with every bite. Fuchsia knew the revulsion Hazel felt when she smelled fresh horse dung, or the thrill when a raccoon got into the house. Best of all, though, were Hazel's dreams. When night fell, and her conscious mind rested, wondrous things crept out from hiding.

There was the woman made of golden glass, transparent, with a locket for a heart. This golden woman was tall, and she would sing lullabies to Hazel. *Baa, baa black sheep, have you any wool? Hey diddle diddle, the cat and the fiddle. Ladybird, ladybird. Mary, Mary, quite contrary.* Sometimes, she would sing other songs, songs that Fuchsia half-remembered. *Amazing Grace. Swing low, sweet chariot.* The golden woman's voice was soothing. Hazel always smiled when she heard it. She and the golden woman would play with rag dolls that could dance unassisted and put on elaborate plays. Sometimes, field mice in clothes—top hats, dresses, bonnets—would come to watch. The plays didn't really make any sense. Fuchsia just enjoyed the warm feeling that suffused these moments.

There was the dream of the dollhouse that floated in the clouds. It had eight gabled roofs the color of red clay and the outer walls were painted pale yellow, the color of fresh butter. Inside, the walls were covered in wallpaper patterned with tiny scarlet and yellow flowers. There was furniture made of dark, sturdy wood: several tables, all dressed in lace, a library full of miniature leather volumes, and a bedroom dominated by a four-poster, canopied bed full of soft pillows. Hazel was the only person in this dollhouse who soared through the sky, always chasing the dawn or the sunset. This was the place where the girl just rested. It was a sanctuary, not unlike the beautiful wetlands Fuchsia had left behind.

Not all of these dreams were halcyon. In fact, the first time she transpierced Hazel, she fell into a fever dream. It was like drowning. After the tranquil beauty of the wetlands, this was a fiery hell. In the grip of illness, Hazel saw blurred things, faces that bled from their eyes and noses. Eyes that were all pupil, or all red-veined whites. She/they saw mouths that were caves, abysses. Rotten teeth yellow and black, gums the color of guano. They smelled the bitter acridity of laudanum, the salt sourness of sweat, the sweet fecal odor of decay. And they saw needles and syringes of glass and metal, raining down on timid brown skin, bruising it black.

There was a moment when Fuchsia thought that she was going to die, as she was spiritually yoked to the child. But gradually, days or hours, the fever subsided in a molasses-slow crawl. The fire in Hazel's veins cooled, became embers. And everything she saw was haloed by a hazy shimmer. Faces looked normal, more or less.

Since then, Hazel would occasionally have a full-on nightmare. Eyeless men, the color of flour and with teeth like glass, would hunt her down in an endless corridor full of holes and rusted nails. Hazel had a fear of snakes. Slit-eyed and fanged, serpents would slither into her shoes, her pinafore pockets, underneath her bonnet. Then there was the nightmare with the golden woman, where the eyeless white men took her away from Hazel. Their claw-like hands dragged the golden woman away. It was heartbreaking, Hazel's tear-streaked face, the imploring stance as they pulled her away.

Hazel would sometimes startle awake during these dark episodes. Upon awakening, the images would fade away. She would forget her nightmares. Fuchsia, however, remembered every image with crystal-clear clarity. The puckered pink flesh of the white demons, the black gums from which their glass-shard teeth grew. Hazel was enslaved. Fuchsia *knew* that the golden woman was some maternal figure in Hazel's life, dimly remembered. During the rare moments when Hazel's mind stilled, she could catch glimpses of the girl's past. Fuchsia saw the coastal South Carolina mansion, its majestic rice plantations, the brown bodies attending the golden husks of grass that grew in muddy channels, sweating in the unforgiving sun. She heard, rather than saw, a motherly figure, in the background. Sweeping a wooden floor, feeding Hazel crackling pork and johnnycakes with honey. The woman didn't have a clear face, but Hazel remembered the swish of her skirts, and how she smelled of mint-scented water. How Hazel got here, on Maryland's Eastern Shore, was unknown.

***

"You black hellion!" said Mrs. Whitby, her face the color of a tomato.

Hazel stood over the shattered remains of a soup tureen.

"I'm sorry, ma'am," she said. She looked down at the floor, the scattered shards.

"Why must you be so careless," Mrs. Whitby continued.

The platter Hazel had broken was "genuine porcelain from China." Furthermore, it was a "gift from a dear, dear friend." The blue and white platter showed gnarled willow trees and women in odd dresses, carrying parasols. It was a pretty scene, and a shame that she had broken it. But it was worth it; Hazel was sure that she wouldn't be on kitchen duty in the near future. How she hated tending the fire and lifting boiling vats of delicious things that she would never be able to eat. "It was so slippery!" she exclaimed. (Hazel deliberately exaggerated her pronunciation; white people loved that.) She immediately burst into hysterical tears, dropping to her knees and throwing in a couple of "Lordy lordys" for good measure. That stopped the worst of the beating Mrs. Whitby gave her. (And frankly, Mrs. Whitby's blows were as soft as a baby's punch.)

The Missus banished her from the kitchen, exiling her to work on clothes, mending them. Needlework was Hazel's passion. She had gotten quite good at it, too. She could thread needles in her sleep, and sewing was a time when she didn't have to be on her feet. She could forget that she was the youngest slave in a house run by fairy tale tyrants.

Master Whitby drank too much, and when he was drunk, he was mean. His were cold rages, given to cruel, cutting remarks. She remembered a recent exchange he'd had with Caleb, the house steward. Master Whitby been mucking about the ledger figures, muttering aloud adding or subtracting some mathematical figure. Caleb, who had lived as a freeman for a number of years, had over-heard Master Whitby murmur the equation out loud. He provided his master with the correct answer to whatever the sum was.

That was a mistake. Whitby had also been nipping at the brandy. The look he'd given Caleb was chilling.

"You know, boy, I can't stand an arrogant nigger." (Caleb was maybe fifteen years older than Whitby.)

"Master Whitby, I'm afraid I don't understand your meaning," Caleb had said, his face respectfully downcast, his body in a sub-missive stance.

"You think you're smarter than me, on account of your educa-tion."

"I do not, sir."

"You're a damn liar."

Caleb wisely didn't respond.

"I said, you're a liar, boy."

"Is there anything else you would like, sir?"

Whitby let Caleb leave, snarling and muttering under his breath.

Mrs. Whitby was a dithering mess of a woman. She was so high-strung that Hazel thought that it would be better if *she* nipped some of the Master's brandy. Helena Whitby was always finding invisible dust on furniture, or stains no one else could see. Judith told Hazel that Missus wasn't fond of the Eastern Shore, with its unpredictable floods and swarms of nits and chiggers that swirled around the marsh. She had come from Boston, and was more comfortable with city living. The relentless damp affected her "delicate constitution."

The couple's children, fifteen-year-old Nathaniel and eighteen-year-old Viktor were the rough and tumble sort, always getting into trouble in town for gambling and liquor. Judith, with whom she shared a room, told her not to complain. There were some slave masters who horse-whipped their niggers, and did even worse things to slave women. The Whitbys were relatively benign.

Maybe that was so, but she still hated them the same.

Hazel took a basket of laundry that needed repairs up to the attic. It was cooler than the rest of house, but Hazel didn't care. She was guaranteed not be disturbed up here among the Whitbys' castoff possessions. She sat on an old wooden chair, and wrapped herself in dusty, moth-eaten shawl and got to work.

An hour or more passed as she mended an assortment of socks, handkerchiefs, bonnets, petticoats and trousers.

Hazel took a break, stood and stretched. She cracked her knuckles, which were stiff. Her eyes fell upon the oddities stored up here. There were old toys, including a pewter whirligig, an old tin drum, a box of marbles, and a rocking horse covered in dust. There was a pile of yellowed linen: tablecloths and napkins.

A crate was filled with papers, doubtlessly old ledgers that Hazel couldn't read anyway. A quick glance showed that at least the top paper was a drawing of some kind. She saw color, and odd shapes. She found herself riffling through the crate. She felt something flutter—a butterfly tremble behind her eyes, in her brain.

To her surprise, the papers were pictures. She'd never seen anything like them. All of the pictures were of flowers. Or, maybe, it was the same flower. It was a weird looking thing, this flower, with petals that looked like misshapen bells. This flower, sphere-like, had antennae sticking out of the bell-like ends, giving it an odd, insectile look. But the thing that made Hazel sure that it was a flower was the color of the petals.

She'd only seen that color once. There had been a fancy Christmas party last year. A young woman guest had worn a dress that color, not quite pink, or purple. The young woman herself wasn't particularly remarkable. She was tanner than most of the ladies at the affair; apparently she was visiting from one of the islands in the Caribbean, where the sun was especially harsh on white skin. Hazel recalled her name: Letitia. Unfortunately, Miss Letty (as they called her) wasn't very nice to anyone (including the hosts), complaining of the rich food that didn't agree with her. She had diarrhea that evening (Hazel had had to empty endless chamber pots full of Miss Letty's excretions). But Hazel always remembered that dress, with its graceful folds of fabric, and especially, that peculiar hue.

As she flipped through the stack of ink drawings—all of which featured the flower in different settings, mostly the scary marsh Judith was always telling her to avoid—time slipped by. The thing was, when she looked at the images—the blue water, the fat fingers of cattail grass, and, of course, that marvelously weird flower—it was like she was actually *in* the marsh. And the marsh wasn't scary at all. It was beautiful and serene. Hazel felt the languid water beneath her finger tips, and heard the weird cries of marsh birds in the distance.

It felt real, like a half-remembered dream. She felt that she recognized this tranquil landscape of billowing grasses, murky waters and endless blue skies. And the flower, that glowed on the paper, firefly bright, was deeply familiar.

But, how was that possible? She had never been in the marsh, had been expressly warned against going there.

She gathered up the drawings, and put them in the basket, beneath the linens.

***

Fuchsia shuddered when Hazel saw the drawings. For weeks or months, she'd been dormant inside the girl. Somehow, she had managed to shut out the onslaught of chatter and images that volleyed through the adolescent's mind. She was only dimly aware of the emotional atmosphere, the rages and frustrations, and the various ever-evolving mood storms. She'd managed to eke out a relatively quiet space, an oasis in Hazel's sentience. Fuchsia had curled herself up small, like a fetus or a seed. She would only expand during the night, when she could roam the gallery of the girl's mind.

But when Hazel caught sight of those drawings, she quivered awake.

The flowers captured on paper and India ink jogged her memory. She knew that she had drawn them. She recalled crouching over the paper in candlelight, shaping the petals and then etching the landscape into existence.

For one briefly, glorious moment, she controlled Hazel. It was clumsy and disorienting, but she made her obey her impulse. Fuchsia flooded her with purpose, and transferred her desire.

It was a small victory, one she cherished, as Hazel's babbling brook of a mind rushed back in.

10: XAVIER

"How's the research going?" Iris asked. She placed a plate of spaghetti slathered with marinara sauce and two golf ball-sized meatballs in front of him. The garlic bread and salad were already on the table.

"It's going well enough," Xavier replied. "I don't know how that museum stays open, though. Many days, I'm the only one there."

"I have no idea," she said. Her face was blank and noncommittal. She sat down with her own laden plate.

So, it's going to be like that, Xavier thought. He'd given it much consideration, how he would approach this subject. The museum archive had scant information on Tamar Dupré, not even a birthdate. A couple of her pieces hung in the Descendants' gallery, a small alcove of artists who had been inspired by Hazel's and Shadrach's work. One piece, "Dark Muse," had the head of a young black woman behind a sheet of white tissue paper on which a marsh-bell was drawn. The stem was a green marker of some sort, and the blossom head was an explosion of glue and glitter. The second piece was a layered collage made of marbleized paper and magazine cut-outs. It was entitled "Sanctuary." Both of these pieces were listless next to the ones in the bin downstairs. When Iris retired for the night, he snuck down to the basement an hour or two afterward and examined the Dupré oeuvre, struck by how powerfully they affected him. The colors popped, and the flowers and faces seemed to live beyond their temporarily frozen moments. He felt he understood the thing that Dupré was trying to express. The flowers and the women somehow fed off each other, in a symbiotic fashion. Marsh biomes were full of such biological relationships, some beneficial and some parasitical. The marsh-muse was somewhere in between that paradigm.

He could imagine Dr. Devine castigating him. "Don't be so timid!" An opportunity presented itself after dinner.

"Care for an after-dinner drink?" Iris said. "I used to be a bartender. Back in the day."

"Sure," Xavier said, "but don't make it too strong."

"Okeydokey," she said with a playful salute. He watched as she made some concoction out of Bourbon, sugar and bitters.

"What's the story of the picture in my room?" he asked as she peeled an orange. "The one above my bed?"

"That was a gift from a close friend of mine," she replied. Her voice was neutral. Was she being evasive? He couldn't tell.

She handed him a glass filled with amber-brown liquid with a peel of orange floating in it. Xavier eyed the drink suspiciously. He wasn't a fan of dark liquor. It reminded him of the endless parties he had to go to with his parents; all of the adults' breath smelled of whiskey and brandy. He preferred sweeter, 'girly' drinks with fruit flavors and umbrellas.

"Is that right?" he said. "It looks awfully similar to one of the artists' work in the museum."

She sipped her cocktail. Her eyes looked away from him, to somewhere distant. She said, still not looking at him, "Of course, *you* would notice that. Tamar and I…"

Her voice wavered a bit. He waited a moment. Iris continued, her voice steadying. "Tamar and I lived together. This used to be her house. Well, her father's house."

"When did she pass?" he asked with what he hoped was the appropriate amount of softness. He'd been hoping that she was still alive so that he could interview her.

"A year ago. But she moved away five years ago, to her aunt's house in Oakland. Her aunt was getting up there in years, so she had to take care of her. We'd lived together, here, for a number of years."

"I'm sorry to hear that." He paused. "I hope that I'm not imposing too much on you, but since I am studying the Shimmer Artists, it would help me if you tell me a little about her."

"Of course I'll help you. I don't know what sort of information you're looking for."

He smiled at her, while internally he had a bit of a nerdgasm. "Why don't you start with how you met Tamar Dupré."

"We met at a restaurant in Baltimore at the time, a fancy place called the Orchid Lounge," Iris began, "one of those real trendy late '90s places. You know the type. Everything had a sauce that was drizzled oh-so-artfully on square white plates. And the desserts came in towers. Pink and black was the main color scheme. Tamar was the hostess there, and I was the bartender. By the way, how do you like your drink?"

He took a sip. It had a nice, smoky flavor free of the alcohol sting he expected. "It's good."

"The Orchid Lounge specialized in frilly, floral drinks. Stuff with rosewater and violet liquors, or drops of grenadine. The signature cocktail was bright pink and had a floating orchid petal on it. Anyway, I'm glad you like the drink. I prefer more old-timey stuff myself.

"I had been working at the Lounge for couple of months when Tamar came on. I don't believe in love at first sight. But she was so beautiful. She had loosely curled hair, smooth skin. She always wore a pink orchid in her hair. Even after she stopped working at the Lounge…"

Iris's voice grew distant and she looked away from him. Maybe she saw Tamar Dupré as she had been. Her voice began to slur, slightly.

"We started dating a month or so later. She was the one who convinced me to do readings. She was into all of that mystical stuff, much more than I ever was. She studied horoscopes like she was studying for the bar. And she could guess your sign and be correct. It was eerie, how accurate she was. I asked her, 'What made you interested in this stuff?'

"She told me that when she was ten or so, she had been a child prophet at a small church in a small town in Carolina. Don't know if it was South or North. Her daddy was the reverend there. Once or twice a month, she put on a show. She'd fall out on the floor of the church and babble nonsense. 'It started off as baby talk,' she told me, 'just repetitive gurgling sounds. Abba-dabba, gaga-goo-goo sounds. The better I got at it, the more complex the sounds I could make, until it actually sounded like a language.' After thrashing around, she would become statue still, and announce that she had been visited by an angel. 'I would pass on their prayers to the angel,' Tamar said.

"Tamar said she did this because her father told her to. Tamar loved her father and would have done anything for him. It all started when she'd seen a woman catch the Spirit once, and she'd imitated her so well that her daddy thought she had real talent. The first few times she did her speaking-in-tongues act had been an experiment, a way to encourage attendance.

"'Weren't you worried that you were pulling the wool over the congregation's eyes?' I asked her.

"'No,' she said. 'Daddy told me that people needed to see miracles every now and then. It couldn't all be about studying the scripture.' And besides, what harm could it do? Tamar wasn't the only holy-roller in that congregation. She was just the most popular one.

"But eventually, it got out of hand. 'Word about me talking to an angel spread around, and soon our tiny church got filled with out-of-towners, hoping for a chance to see me. It was standing room only. I had people telling me, an eleven-year-old, about their sick children, or cheating husbands. Women would weep, men would beg me for grace. It was frightening. I told Daddy that I wanted to stop, but he wouldn't let me. He told me that I was doing such good work, I had such talent. So I continued.'

"Tamar Dupré became the face of the Supreme Light. The congregation grew, and eventually, they moved to a bigger church. She appeared on a couple of regional television shows. She even showed me a video tape of one of her appearances."

"What was that like?" Xavier asked. By this time, he had drunk half of the Old-Fashioned, and he could feel the lazy golden coil of intoxication unwinding in him.

"It was insane," said Iris. "Tamar had an old VHS, so it wasn't the best quality. Plus, the camera work was strictly amateur. You know, shaky shots and really bad lighting."

"*Blair Witch*-style."

"Yeah. In the video, Tamar goes into one of her trances. Even though I knew she was faking it, it still looked creepy as hell. Her eyes rolled up into her head and she began to utter a whole lot of nonsense, like 'Shambalalalala.' But the expression on her face was what sold the act. It was somewhere between terror and joy. I didn't know if she was screaming in pain or singing for joy. Tamar fell backwards, into her daddy's arms after a long string of syllables. When she opened her eyes, her face was empty. She looked like a doll, with her blank expression. She just stared and stared at the camera as if she was looking just at you...."

Xavier imagined a pretty little girl, dressed in a stiff lace dress with ribbons in her hair glaring coldly at him.

Iris continued: "Anyway. Tamar told me that her days as a child prophet ended abruptly when an undercover news reporter did an exposé on the Church of Supreme Light, revealing that her daddy never went to seminary and had a criminal history. She told me that she was glad that her child prophet days were over.

"'There was one moment where I actually felt something enter me, during one of my performances,' she said. 'I felt someone else's thoughts intruding on mine. I saw fragments of things, faces, places that I'd never seen before. Words and images slipped over my own. It felt like one song was playing over another one. Nothing made sense.'"

Iris paused here. Both of their glasses were empty.

She said, "That's what got her interested in all of that otherworldly stuff. She was frightened, but also, curious."

"When did she start making art?"

"When we moved to Shimmer. Her father had moved up here years ago. He managed to eke out a living as a waterman. But that's hard living, and his health began to fail. Tamar quit her job at the Orchid Lounge and moved up here. When I was laid off a few months later, I did, too. It wasn't smooth sailing, though. He wasn't crazy about his daughter being a lesbian. I remember overhearing a fight between them one night. Tamar said to him, 'Who has the criminal record in this house?' That shut him up. About *that* issue. But Ernest Dupré was a miserable sonafabitch, especially when he developed dementia….

"Tamar started making her collages after Ernest died. At first, it was just a couple of pieces a week. At the time, I had another bartending job in Ocean City, so I wasn't really around. After Ernest died, she spent her time settling his estate and dealing with the probate court. I remember asking her about them. She just said it was therapeutic. Something to do, busywork. That sort of thing. Then I began to see more and more of them.

"All of them were the same—an image of a flower or of a woman.

Sometimes the two together. Or one *hiding* in the other. That's when I began to think that it was a little odd. You could say that she was obsessed. Then I saw her making one of them."

She frowned, remembering something.

"She cut out all sorts of flower pictures. Roses, daffodils, jonquils. Flowers of all colors and shapes. But when she put them on the pasteboard, they turned into the marsh-bell orchid. They turned magenta, changed shape."

Xavier thought, *This woman is crazy. She must be drunk.* At the same time, Iris looked sincere.

He said, "Wow." He hoped that he didn't come across as condescending.

"You don't believe me," Iris said. "That's okay. I know what I saw."

The night had ended on a sour note. Xavier made a quick exit, telling her that he needed to start work early. When he turned off the light, he saw a flare of magenta from the picture above his bed. A flower-shaped explosion of color. It burned in the air and faded away. It was probably just the afterimage of the lightbulb, nothing more.

11: FUCHSIA (1843)

At first, Fuchsia just focused on Hazel's dreams. Her babbling-brook mind slowed down to a trickle then, and it was easier to float images on to the stream. Nothing too complex or even well-formed. She flashed the birds she saw, the hawks, herons, the occasional eagle. They soared in the sleeping child's mind, borne on the wind of dreams.

***

"Boo!" said Jethro. He had snuck up behind her. His laughter interrupted her focus and startled the hawk that had been perched on the tree that she had been studying. It flew up, brown and white stippled wings flapping towards the marsh.

"Why'd you do that?" said Hazel. "You scared him away."

"Scared who? That bird? I did no such thing. He was probably hungry, and went out looking for a rat or something." Jethro could be annoying. Recently, he'd taken to teasing her. He would seek out the places where she hid away and chatter inanely to her. His jokes weren't funny. He'd tell her about the horses in the stable, or some town gossip, stuff she didn't care about.

"Boy, quit playing!" she said.

"*I'm* not the one looking at birds when they should be straightening up the bedrooms," he replied. He crooked an eyebrow at her.

"What are you? A snitch? Stop minding me. I *know* you have work of your own to mind." She scowled at him until he left. To her irritation, he started whistling happily as he trudged to the stables.

The thing was, Jethro was partially correct. The past few weeks, she had been distracted. Judith had snapped at her to pay attention to her work. Missus had called her a "lazy pickaninny, always underfoot." Even Caleb had taken her aside, telling, "Best do your work, gal. This house ain't as bad as some of them other plantations. In fact, we're blessed. The Crosbys whip their niggers if they don't make their quotas. One of the sons had his way with a couple of house niggers, whelped a few mulattos. I'm telling you this because as comfortable as you might feel here, you—or I—could be sold at a whim. Stay useful. Indispensable. We're only 'family' to them when we work hard."

But she couldn't help it. Night and day, and all hours in between, she was bombarded with stray thoughts that she had no control over. She might suddenly see birds in her mind's eye. All kinds of them, from elegant herons with their needle-thin beaks to brown-tailed hawks that soared on thermals. She'd think of their feather patterns, the color of their eyes, the shape of their bodies. She wanted—needed—to capture their essence, somehow. She had even found herself drawing simple shapes in the mud. Hazel knew that she even dreamed about these things. She'd wake up with bright images in her brain. Ruffled feathers, clouds, intensely blue skies, awe-inspiring swoops and peaceful glides. Hazel had no idea where this sudden passion for the natural world came from.

Sometimes, it terrified her. She knew the names of things with no particular education. While Caleb tutored the Whitby boys, he was expressly forbidden to teach any of the other slaves anything. Hazel couldn't read, but certain words appeared in her brain suddenly, for no reason. One evening, as the sun set, she knew that the sky was a *cerulean* color. She had never heard the word spoken. But it wrote itself on her mind. She could almost see the shape of the letters. And the word so was rich, so musical—it had a pool in the middle of it. A pool of dark blue. *Ce-rooool-lian.* The R rolled like water tumbling from a fountain. Flowers weren't just red or purple or blue. She knew the names of the various shades. Carmine, vermillion, violet, robin's egg blue. The world around her suddenly became more alive, bursting with hidden knowledge.

This new knowledge filled her up. She wanted to share it, somehow. Spill it out to the air. To spread it out. Tell people that flower wasn't just blue, it was *periwinkle*. That leaf wasn't just green, it was *peridot*. At first, she shared her color knowledge with the other servants. When she informed Judith that one of the Missus's dresses was *coral*, and not just pink, Judith had given her an odd look. And she told Jethro that the Master's stallion wasn't just brown; it was *chestnut*. He accused her of "putting on airs." "You just a nigger, like me," he'd said in huff.

One afternoon, when Master Whitby was away in town, she was in his study, ostensibly to straighten it up. His desk was a mess. Papers and books were strewn across it, along with the stale crusts of bread and a full ashtray. She carefully stacked the books and arranged the papers into neat piles after clearing the polished cherrywood desk of crumbs. In the desk drawer, there were a couple of old fountain pens, half-full bottles of black ink and sheets of new white paper. Hazel snatched one of the bottles, the ink, and a pen. She buried them beneath her basket of cleaning rags. She knew Viktor Whitby wouldn't miss a bottle or a few sheets of paper. He was a drunk.

***

Fuchsia was certain that Hazel wouldn't get in trouble for the small theft. Mostly certain. Vague memories stirred, like slow dust motes in a ray of sunshine. She remembered always cleaning some white people's messes. Minding their babies, their linens, their lives. The monotonous drudgery. The way white folks thought you were barely human, more like a talking mule to be used. She had lived in a house like the Whitbys' once, long ago. She knew that life had been unbearable, full of casual cruelty. A Negro boy at that house of long ago had once stolen something, maybe one of the white children's toys. He'd been whipped like a horse. The red gashes and welts, his squealing like a pig being slaughtered still haunted her.

No. She would not remember that life. That life was gone, over. She forgot her name. It was a willful act. She drowned it in the marsh, beneath the muddy waters. When she rose again, in her fuchsia finery, she left that name and that history behind. It was washed away, like silt and fishbones. She let her memories evaporate like mist.

The child's life was wasted here, as a less-than-human thing to be used by cold and indifferent white folks. Just as her former life had been. Fuchsia wanted to show Hazel that life was not just endless droning service to people who could have you killed at a whim. The pen, the paper, the ink were all keys, ones that could open a door to new possibilities.

Hazel made marks on the paper whenever she had a spare moment, mostly in the evenings. Her motor skills and unfamiliarity with penmanship made for awkward, shaky strokes. Once, she even spilled ink on her dress. Luckily, she had a pinafore to cover up the stain. Each time she picked up the pen was a failure. It was unwieldy in her hands, and Fuchsia could feel the swell of frustration in Hazel. She was a stubborn child at the best of times. Eventually, she returned the stolen pen to its desk, and managed to quash Fuchsia's influence, for a while.

***

It was a struggle to get through the day without being distracted. Hazel threw herself into her work, giving every task her undivided attention. Even things she hated, like laundry, or darning socks. She became a model worker, something that even the sour Missus noticed. She even said thank you to her every once in a while. Hazel learned to make bread, how to garden, and how to make soap. She mopped the floors daily, trimmed the candlewicks, and started long neglected projects, like polishing the silver. She sang while she worked, scraps of lullabies or work songs she heard when she passed the plantations on the way to town.

Caleb complimented her good, Christian work ethic. She was proud of herself, in a way. She kept the thing within her hidden and more importantly, quiet. Not that the presence didn't flare up every now and then. There were moments in the day when she was bombarded with images. Blue water. Brown reeds. Wading herons. And, most prominently, strange purple flowers. No, not purple. *Fuchsia*. The word rolled around in her brain like a marble. She loved the sound it made, the way it whispered at the end. The flower, a slender stalk festooned with a sphere of bell-like blossoms, bloomed in her dreams. There were so many bells on each flower. Maybe fifty, maybe a hundred per plant. It grew on wet hillocks, in between strands of marsh grass, where it fed on fungal spores. Sometimes, she saw the shape of the flower, its wide bell-mouths sucking her soul inside. Other times, she would see just flashes of color, bright spots that burned long after she'd seen them, on her hands, on any surface where her eyes just happened to land.

Was she going mad? Once, during a trip to town, she'd seen a mad white woman roaming the streets, her clothes impossibly filthy, her bonnet more grey than white. She'd been taking to someone who wasn't visible and twitching. She'd been with the Missus then, and the Missus said, "Poor thing, kicked out of her family. Madness just creeps up on people, like a curse. One day, you wake up seeing things that aren't there, talking to invisible things."

She didn't hear voices. At least, not yet. But she had the feeling that the flashes of color, flowers and birds were a message of some kind. Who was sending the message? And what did it mean?

***

Fuchsia was trapped inside the girl. Days blended together. Weeks passed. The child became a woman when her monthlies started. She was no longer strong enough to affect Hazel one way or another, at least when she was awake. Hazel's adolescent changes trampled Fuchsia's feeble suggestions. Hazel was a raging river; Fuchsia was just a single reed always on the verge of being uprooted.

Entering Hazel was a mistake. What had she been thinking? Fuchsia saw herself as an essence, a mist. A will-o'-the-wisp that lived in the Shimmer Marsh. She should have stayed far from flesh and blood, from humanity. She would fade away, yoked to this soul.

***

A low fog hugged the ground, blurring everything. Hazel was on the porch, waiting for the sunrise. She'd been having trouble sleeping for the last couple of days. Her nights were punctuated by sudden, disturbing images. Petals on water, sinking. A girl in a bright purple-pink gauze beneath the water, dead but with her eyes wide open. Burning marshes, orbs of glowing color. Things that made no sense. The dreams were fleeting and intense, like sudden downpours. Images flooded her head, swirling around until she woke up.

Hazel told no one about her nightmares. Who was there to tell? The Whitbys were cool and distant to each other, let alone to their inferiors. Caleb the steward was loyal to the family and took his duties very seriously. Judith was cautious and conservative, and she didn't trust Jethro. Hazel was alone. And what would she tell someone, anyway? She was too old for this kind of nonsense.

She'd brought up a basket of fabric scraps and her needles. It was too early to do her chores, so she had a vague intention to do some quilting. She needed a new bedspread anyway, and more importantly, it was busywork. The torrent of images hadn't bothered her in the daytime for a long while. Hazel thought that they could start up again at any time.

The basket was full of odds and ends. There was an old blue dress, a couple of calico-printed flour sacks, and some earth-colored work trousers. Hazel tried to see if she could somehow patch them together into something harmonious. It would surely be one ugly quilt, with its mixture of fabrics. She sighed. Negroes weren't allowed finer things. They got hand-me-downs, and the cuts of meat considered too coarse for white palates.

She started cutting up the blue dress into more manageable strips. The fabric was soft, probably Merino wool. The color was beautiful, a deep blue that reminded her of the bay's water on certain days.

The idea for the quilt hit her like a lightning strike. Blue water, brown reeds. And bright petals. A marsh grew beneath her fingers.

***

And suddenly, Hazel's fingers were Fuchsia's fingers. She had hands again, and eyes and muscle memory. Hazel couldn't draw. However, she could sew. Stitches could shape worlds, just as well as pens.

Hazel cut out the rough shapes of trees and flowers. Muddy hillocks, drifting grasses. Fuchsia fed her the images, and the colors.

Hazel was, of course, interrupted frequently from her work. She had to do her chores. She did them quickly, making sure not to make any mistakes. Then she went back to quilting whenever she could spare a moment or two.

Ten days later, after a couple of sleepless nights, the quilt was finished.

Mostly finished. Something was missing. It had most of the colors of the Shimmer Marsh, the blue, the brown and the green. But one color was missing. One shape.

Hazel cut out the shape from the blue dress, fully intending it to be the woman who appeared in her dreams. It turned into a flower, but the color was all wrong.

Fuchsia was her name. Her name was a color. Color was also a sound, a song. All color was made of other colors, other songs. She added the song of bright red to the gentle blue song of the marsh waters. Red, like a cardinal's feathers, leaves in autumn, of rage and blood. Red, intertwined with blue, gradually staining the fabric flowers the color of her name.

12: LINCOLN

Working at the museum was the best job Linc had gotten so far during his exile on the Eastern Shore. He was a combination security guard, maintenance man, and, on occasion, a tour guide. Not that the Whitby-Grayson Museum was particularly busy. The most people he'd seen in the building for the three weeks he worked here was a group of ten. He wondered how it managed to stay open.

"Eugenia Fraser is the one who opened the museum," Howard told him. "She was the heiress to Fraser Fisheries. She collected both Hazel's quilts and Shadrach's paintings back in the 1960s. The museum was constructed in the '90s to house her collection. It stays open through her endowment."

He'd shown Linc a picture of Fraser. By the '90s she was elderly, maybe in her late seventies. She had been a tall woman with a striking sense of style. With her silver hair in a short, spiky cut and a tailored pinstripe pantsuit, she could have been a fixture in the New York art scene. "She thought that Hazel and Shadrach were overlooked Outsider Artists."

"Forgive my ignorance, but what exactly is an 'Outsider Artist'?"

"It's a kind of umbrella term. In a broad sense, they are visual artists who have no formal training. In particular, though, they are people who create things because of some compulsion. They often view their work as messages or portals. In other words, what they make has a meaning beyond just being displayed."

There were, roughly speaking, two main types of visitors to the museum, the Quilters and the Ghost Hunters. Groups of middle-aged African-Americans came to pay homage to Hazel's work. Most of them were fellow quilters coming to marvel at Whitby's work. These women were respectful and followed the museum's rules (no photographs). They would spend hours carefully discussing each and every tapestry. They marveled over the artistry and original-ity. For the most part, they ignored Grayson's work and the small gallery dedicated to other artists inspired by Whitby and Grayson. The other audience was made up of hipsters. Girls in baby doll dresses, Ugg boots and oversized sunglasses. Men with scraggly beards, skinny jeans and porkpie hats. They mostly gravitated to-wards Grayson's work, its stark, sea-washed landscapes dominated by glowing fuchsia orbs.

He once overheard a group of them theorizing about Shadrach Grayson: "I think he was on drugs of some kind. Like, datura," one porkpie hat wearer said. The cadence of his deep voice suggested that *he* was under the influence of something or other.

A girl with an asymmetrical haircut that was dyed a dandelion-yellow replied, "You say that about all abstract art. Rothko was on hallucinogens. Leonora Carrington did opium. That's such weak sauce."

"Okay, then Ms. *Art Forum*. Why do you think he painted those orbs?"

"I don't know. But I read somewhere that Grayson was directed to paint by a spirit of some kind."

"A g-g-g ghost?"

"Very funny. Besides, it doesn't matter whether or not there actu-ally was a ghost. Grayson believed that there was one."

In each group, there was always at least one person who was either unimpressed ("It looks like a kid could do it,") or downright disturbed ("Those paintings make me want to take a Dramamine!"). Linc went back and forth on Whitby vs. Grayson. Whitby's flowers that were sometimes women (or, a woman) were a little dizzying. Grayson's glowing orbs were calming, save in the way the color seemed to luminesce with some secret fire. By his third week, he no longer found the paintings and tapestries either creepy or enthralling. Instead, they were comforting.

There were long stretches of time when he was alone with the artwork. He got used to their erratic behavior. The dancing balls of light, the shifting images were soothing, and it had been a long time since he had felt good just being in the moment.

***

"I'll see you tomorrow," said Howard. He had his coat and hat on, flexed his umbrella since there was a downpour. He had a doctor's appointment, so he had to leave early that day. "You have my number if you have any problems closing up."

"See ya," Linc replied, and Howard went out into the misty windy outdoors. This was the first time he'd been alone in the building. Howard was always there when he got to work in the morning. He hovered around Linc as he did his rounds, as if he didn't quite trust him. Linc supposed that it was to be expected, him being new to the job, but Lenski was disquieting.

He was always straightening things, the brochures that almost no one touched, putting trashcans at the proper angle, checking if the tapestries and paintings were level. Lenski worked in the back office, but he would come out at least once an hour to pace and cast sly, supervisory glances at Linc. For his part, Linc tried to stay busy, but, frankly, there was only so much busy work he could do.

Lenski never engaged in small talk, but he could rattle off information about the artwork like he was a walking encyclopedia. Linc privately referred to Lenski as WikiMan. The man was a walking hyperlink.

When Howard Lenski left the museum, it felt like the atmosphere inside changed. The tension in the room disappeared, and left with the man into the rain. Linc felt his muscles relax. He exhaled. He had at least three hours before he closed the museum, three hours of solitude. Probably there would be no visitors; the torrential rains were supposed to last well into the evening.

There were three galleries in the building. The main one housed Whitby's tapestries. The second one was Grayson's. The third gallery was smaller and featured artists inspired by the two of them. He was well-acquainted with the first two rooms. He slipped back into the third gallery, with the self-justification that he should know everything about the museum. He wouldn't be in there long, anyway. And if there was a visitor, he could hear them enter. The acoustics of the museum were echoey and cavernous.

None of the other artists' work was as compelling as Whitby's or Grayson's. But they used the fuchsia hue or images of the marshbell. Most of it was amateurish, primitive folk art. One woman, Bathsheba Upchurch, repurposed church banner material, felt and Velcro. Her church banners had bright marsh-bells stuck against white satin banners, arranged like notes in a staff. There were two of them mounted on the wall. Linc read the bio stenciled next to the art.

Bathsheba Upchurch's art was found in the church basement, hidden among the items for an upcoming White Elephant sale. Bathsheba spent most of her free time at Trinity Methodist, serving on many committees and prayer groups. Her work was covered by a dusty tarp, reportedly sandwiched between a rack of dresses and an old bookcase.

Bathsheba Davis was born outside of St. Louis. She married young, sixteen years old, to John Upchurch, who was 10 years her senior. They moved to Shimmer sometime in the 1920s. Mr. Upchurch worked as a general laborer at various places, including the stockyards and a bottle factory while Bathsheba raised their 8 children. Not much is known about her, save for the fact that she was devoted to both her family and her church.

James Olds's work was encased in a Lucite block. There were six glass bottles of different shapes and sizes, all decorated in that orchid shade, with painted shells and beads meticulously inlaid like mosaic pieces.

Olds's decorated bottle trees were randomly scattered among his 2-acre property, located on the outskirts of Shimmer. The bottles were all shapes and sizes, ranging from the iconic Coke bottle to milk bottles.

All of the artists lived in Shimmer at one point. There were watercolors, magic marker drawings, and in one case, a series of dolls in fuchsia outfits. Another thing he noticed was that all of the artists had no particular ambition to share their work. The art was found posthumously or hidden. It was eerie.

In the crawlspace beneath the stairs, Edna Wray had built a room inhabited by sixteen porcelain dolls. The room was carpeted, and she had built shelves, on which the dolls sat, arranged around the small room. The dolls were all in various states of disrepair, missing glass eyes or hands. Some of the skulls were cracked open, revealing the hollow insides. A couple of them had burn marks on their clothes. They were all castaways, all of them denuded of hair.

Wray transformed them. Each doll was painstakingly painted or glazed in shades of brown, mimicking the skin tones of African/black skin, from high yellow to blue black, still dressed in satin and silk pet-

ticoats. All female dolls, from babies to little girls, some of them older women. All of the dolls were arranged in a semi-circle, gazing at the center of the room. In the center, Wray had placed a toy flower pot, and growing out of it was a silk and wire orchid, in a magenta/fuchsia shade.

Linc would have stayed in the small gallery for a little while longer, but he heard someone in the main room. He hurried up to the information desk, only to find that no one was actually there. Gusts of wind blew veils of rain out over the marsh. Maybe he had heard something blowing around in that sodden mess.

He pulled out his phone. It was great to have one again. It was a cheap, prepaid phone with limited data. But it could text. He'd gotten it with his first paycheck. It felt nice to be a part of the normal world again. He saw that there was a text from his sister.

—Just checking in. How are you?

—Doing well. Looking for a permanent place 2 live, he texted back.

—You know, I told Mom that U & I were in contact.

Linc's stomach dropped, right into his guts. It took him a moment to work through the storm of emotion that sizzled through his head before replying.

—What did she say?

He held his breath. It was reflexive, this pocket of air trapped, suspended in his lungs.

—She says Daddy and her think about you constantly. They would love to hear from you. They're happy to know you're clean.

Clean. The word, in this context, was repulsive. All the nights he slept in the park, washed up in bus station bathrooms, begged on the streets of DC, Baltimore and Wilmington came back to him. The second skin of grime that washed down the drain of a shelter's shower. Sucking cock, having his own sucked for money,

the horrible passionless orgasmless mechanics of sex for cash. Was
he Clean? No. He was cleaner. But he still felt the stains that no
amount of scrubbing would vanquish.

—I'll send them an email. Even as he texted it, he knew that it
was a lie. Or, at least, a partial lie. He *would* email his folks, just
not now.

—I wish you would tell me where you were, Elaine texted back.
—I could send you some money.

Linc heard footsteps. He looked up from his phone screen, trying
to locate the sound.

"Hello?" he said.

Silence. He paused, listening for more sounds. A minute passed,
two.

—Don't worry about me, he texted Elaine back, —I'm making
decent money.

He heard it again. Feet on poured concrete, the sound muffled
yet reverberating. It came from the small gallery in the back. He
put his phone back into his pocket, and left the information desk.
He knew it was next to impossible for someone to slip by unno-
ticed in the museum. He still felt like a stupid white girl in a horror
movie as he crept through the gallery. Then, as he turned to go
back to the information desk, something moved.

It was instinct that made Linc glance at the three dolls in their
Lucite-walled display case. One of the track lights was focused
on it, flooding their platform with illumination. One of the dolls
was missing an eye. Another one had a crack, straight down its
porcelain face. All of them were glazed with a brown tone, over
their original cream-and-roses complexion. Edna Wray's dolls were
probably the creepiest thing in the collection. Linc stared at them,
waiting. Nothing happened. But as soon as he looked away—

There! Something bright wavered. He looked at the display head
on. The dolls weren't moving, thank God. But their clothes *were*.

Well, the clothes weren't exactly moving. They were rippling, like they were pools of water. A gentle, lulling pulse of fuchsia.

When he'd tweaked on crystal, he'd had hallucinations like these—minor disturbances. Delicate, fractal-like distortions, objects that had momentary animation. He hadn't touched the stuff for months, not since he had left Baltimore and Gash behind. For one second, he was transported back to that dank basement apartment, tweaking as he watched the gelatinous bubbles of a lava lamp drift and form new shapes.

Linc made a decision then, to ignore this visual irritation. Flashbacks weren't a part of crystal addiction. But that didn't mean they were impossible. One of the reasons why he wasn't quite ready to return home was that he didn't trust himself. He didn't know where Gash was, but he was afraid if he saw him again, he would fall back into his old ways. Linc did not crave crystal at all. The initial rush and cascade of euphoria was great, yes, but it came bundled with rage, psychosis, and bone-deep illness. There were days when his nerves felt like strings, taut and ready to be plucked. They were followed by days of darkness, when the strings were snapped and untuned. When sleep could not cure the exhaustion, when even the blood in his veins felt sluggish. What he did crave, though, was sex on crystal.

Sex had always been awkward for Linc. The placement of body parts, the delicate timing, the occasional discomfort, the mess afterwards. When he was on crystal, none of those barriers remained. Everything was amazing, nothing off limits. If some dude wanted to lick his eyelids, then his eyelids became hot-wired sexual organs. He found pleasure in the strangest places. The crooks of elbows, between fingers, behind the ears. If another dude wasn't into foreplay, that was cool. If another one was just into dry humping, Linc could dry hump him for hours. Sex on crystal was intense, euphoric and endless.

But I'm not on crystal anymore, he thought. Then why was he seeing rippling dresses? Linc turned away from the room, went back to the main gallery and sat behind the information desk. Outside, the wind had died down and the rain was steady but no longer pounding.

Linc put on his rain poncho to check on the marsh-bells. They were beneath an awning, spared from the worst of the rain, but the wind still could have done some damage. He fully expected the flowers to be destroyed, the bell-shaped petals scattered across the entrance.

The flowers were intact. Not a bloom askew. They stood up against the wind, without so much as a quiver. It was odd. The winds had been pretty high. According to his phone's weather app, the storm wind's gusts were up to 40mph. But the marsh-bells stood still.

No.

Not still.

The tiny bell-like blossoms rippled with color. Each individual blossom radiated briefly before settling down. It was random, which blossom would glow, which flower, like twinkling Christmas lights.

Gerald said the museum was haunted. Lenski's words came back to Linc. He thought that this was silly. He'd seen some ghost hunter shows on television and it was his personal belief that the 'investigators' freaked themselves out. The flickering plants were an optical illusion, a visual hallucination. Residual detoxification. A flashback. That was all.

He went back inside the museum. He checked his phone.

—I love you, Elaine had texted. White words against a sky-blue text bubble.

"Damn," he said aloud, to no one. Because he was crying. It took a lot for his sister to write those words. He dried his eyes on his sleeve.

When he lifted his face from his forearm, something had changed.

There was the smell of brackish water floating in the air, along with a faint trace of sulfur. Linc heard sounds. No footsteps, but the distant cry of seagulls and the whispering of reeds in the wind. And the fuchsia spots on Whitby's quilts were animated, undulating like the dolls' dresses and the marsh-bells.

The pieces of fabric shifted into flowers, into a vague female shape and back again. Linc knew that this was no flashback. He checked the Shadrach Grayson gallery. The orbs burned like fire, amorphous over their watery landscapes. He could guess the same thing was happening in the other gallery.

Linc wasn't afraid. He was strangely elated, as if he was honest with himself. Weird things didn't happen to him. And this wasn't just weird, it was miraculous. He took pictures and videos of the phenomena with no real plan in place. He did know, however, that he would not show it to Howard Lenksi. That seemed wrong, somehow. The artwork lay dormant when Howard was around, as if his presence suppressed the phantom energy.

The bottles glowed and grew ghostly marsh-bells that faded and regrew. Grayson's orbs detached from the somber background and floated out, spun around the room before returning to their paintings. Linc laughed, maybe for the first time in months.

Then, the spectral hue began to *whisper*.

13: IRIS (1987)

Black Madonna statue was in the window, staring out at the street. Her skin was actually black, the color of charcoal. It contrasted with her sky-blue robe. She was surrounded by a halo, rays of gold leaf. The child she held in one arm, however, was white, with a painted peaches-and-cream complexion and a puff of pale blond hair. The name BOTÁNICA OLOKUN was painted on the window in gold letters in an Art Nouveau style.

This was the kind of place that Pop-Pop would have called heathen. He'd be frowning down at her from Heaven. If she believed in Heaven, or at least his version of it. Still, it was hard to undo years of brainwashing, so Iris felt a tingle of delicious wickedness in the pit of her stomach when she entered the store. The smell of the place was the first thing to hit her. She smelled herbs, patchouli, anise, mint. There were also floral scents, lavender and rose and the smell of cedar and cinnamon. The aisles were full of marvelous things, like candles of all colors and carved statues of saints and rosary beads. She saw a couple of depictions of Jesus, including one with thick dreadlocks. The botánica was such a strange place—both sacred and pagan. Spells and scriptures existed together in this chaotic space.

The store bustled with activity, and she heard voices in Spanish, Portuguese, English and other tongues she couldn't identify. Music drifted down from hidden speakers, a light samba beat with mournful female vocals swooping over it. Iris felt like she was in a foreign country. She made her way up to the register. There was the most beautiful man Iris ever saw milling around the area behind register. His skin was smooth and golden, his hair black, and his eyes were the bright green color of pears. She could see his muscles behind his pale cotton shirt.

"I'm looking for Bastien," she said when she caught his eye.

He smiled. His teeth were perfect. Of course they were. Iris felt flush. At seventeen, she thought that she was no great beauty. She was too short, with no curves whatsoever, and she wore her hair in a short buzz cut. People constantly took her for a boy of ten or eleven. Because of that, she wore skirts, usually without patterns and in solid colors. This gentleman looked like a telenovela star.

"You're speaking to him!" he replied. "You must be Iris. You look a little like Earline."

She smiled at him, hoping that it wasn't a stupid smile.

Bastien called over a woman who was stocking one of the shelves to operate the register. He took Iris into a back room filled with overstock. White saints and black gods peered down on them when the two of them settled into a couple of folding chairs.

Bastien said, "Earline told me a little about your situation. But I want to hear it from you."

"I see things," she began. She checked Bastien's face for any sarcasm or mirth. If there was any, he hid it well beneath a warm and welcoming expression. The lambency in his green eyes compelled to her to continue. "I think that they're ghosts. Dead people. But they're not at all like the ones you see in the movies."

"Hollywood never gets anything right," Bastien said. "Santeros are portrayed as people who spatter chicken blood over everything."

"Like that Lisa Bonet movie?"

"Exactly."

"Well, I don't see transparent people. I don't see people at all. No gory bodies. Nothing like that. I see colors and patterns in the shape of people. Sometimes they are solid, like gold and green. And sometimes they look like paper doll cutouts. All of them glow. And sometimes, it hurts to look at them."

"Everyone sees ghosts differently. Sometimes, it's not seeing at all. It might be scents or sounds."

"I wish I didn't see them. I mean, I've gotten used to it, and can ignore them. But that wasn't always the case. My classmates thought I was odd. A space case. They called me 'Ritzy Ditzy.'"

She wasn't invited to sleepovers and birthday parties. Boys and girls avoided her like she had the plague. Iris became resigned to the fact that she exuded strangeness. Even her teachers were jittery around her. Not that she could blame them. The sudden appearance of glowing silhouettes was hard to get used to, even though she got better at banishing them to her periphery.

Iris went on: "These ghosts or spirits are attracted to me. Like a moth is to a flame. I mean, that's my theory anyway. But they're just there. They don't try and interact with me. Half the time, I wonder if they even see me. Like, the attraction is just an instinct, with no thought to it.

"Then I met Pearl. She is taller than I am. Maybe five-foot-six. She was pale pink, the color of cotton candy. I could tell that she was around my age, maybe a little younger. At first, she appeared in my neighborhood. In the corner store, or in Mercy Park. I didn't think anything of it. I never talk to the spirits. I don't want to encourage them. Eventually, they fade away after a couple days. *She* was persistent. I began to see her every day. For one week. Then two.

"I began to get worried. Because this cotton candy girl was beginning to show up closer and closer to me. In the hallways of school. Waiting for me at the corner.

"By the way, my mother doesn't know about my visions. My grandfather would have disowned me if he had known. Mama's not as religious, but she would definitely disapprove. I'm telling you this because there were a few times when the girl would be around, and Mama would see me glancing at her. At something. This ghost girl was becoming intrusive.

"Finally, one Saturday at Mercy Park, when I was sure no one was around, I asked her what she wanted. I had never really communicated with them. But I needed to know. I don't think I was prepared for an answer.

"She didn't actually speak to me. Thoughts and images flashed in my head. They swirled around in there like snakes. Words, and lightning-quick flashes collided with my own thoughts. It was so sudden and creepy, that I practically ran away from her, from the park. It felt like my head was full of bees. A whole hive of them, droning away. It was horrifying, made me feel nauseous.

"Afterwards, when I saw her, she was different. Cotton candy is just strands of spun sugar, right? Well, now the strands of cotton candy billowed, like a sea of pink clouds. It's like when yeast is activated, you know? Suddenly it bubbles and foams and comes alive. For a couple of days, I lived in sheer terror that she would try and worm her way into my mind."

Bastien said, "That sounds similar to what happens to me when I communicate with the Orishas. When Olokun enters my soul, I see what he sees. I see the dark colors of the sea, and hear the song of the waves in my blood. It can be dizzying."

Iris felt a slight twinge of guilt, speaking openly about things that were blasphemous to her grandfather and her mother. The old gods were demons, as far as they were concerned. Pop-Pop would have called Bastien a witch doctor, if he was still around. She looked up at the god statues, and felt a shudder go through her body. The resin figurines were no longer just objects. Suddenly, they seemed alive and predatory. Was one of these disembodied spirits waiting to take her over?

"I didn't like that feeling. Or, at least, then I didn't. But first I tried a bunch of things to get her to leave me alone."

Iris had tried crucifixes, even hung one in her room. Of course, that didn't work. The cotton candy girl wasn't a vampire. She read somewhere that sage could chase away unwanted spirits. There was a jar of it in the kitchen, so she sprinkled some of it in front of her bedroom door. Mama was a neat freak, though, and it had been swept up by the next day.

"Finally, I had had enough. By this time, she had taken to appearing in my bedroom, a shimmering shape that almost made me want to puke! So, I let her in."

She drowned in a flood of imagery and sounds as before. But since she knew what to expect this time, it wasn't so overwhelming. She saw sand, piers, miles of boardwalk, the gaudy neon lights of hotels, the tumble of black-and-white gull wings, throngs of stumbling, sweat-sheened people and most of all the ever-present expanse of the Atlantic, strips of muddy brown water giving way to deep blue until the horizon. Iris recognized the place the cotton candy girl showed her. Mona had taken her to Atlantic City a few times. She even played quarter slots every once in a while, telling Iris, "This'll just be our little secret." She remembered going down the streets, which had the same names as Monopoly properties.

"It was hard to get a thought in; she just steamrolled over my own thoughts. But eventually, we came upon a method of talking to each other. I would whisper aloud, and she would answer in images."

Over a couple of months, Iris pieced together the rough shape of the cotton candy girl's life. The girl had a strong attachment to Atlantic City, and the ocean in general. She was obsessed with sea shells in particular. Their shapes slithered through Iris's mind. Iris became an expert even though she was miles from the Atlantic. She became familiar with their names and colors. Beaded periwinkle, Paper Fig, the Alphabet Cone. She even began to research them on her own, finding out about the mollusks that discarded these bits of calcium carbonate. Iris gave the cotton candy girl a name: Pearl. When she told her that, Pearl's pinkness flickered from the pale pink of quartz to a deeper rose tone.

"I liked it at first," Iris said. "It was…."

"Intimate," Bastien finished her sentence. He leaned forward.

"Yeah. I mean, I've never been that close to someone before."

Among the onslaught of images Pearl sent her was one of a smooth-skinned young woman with french-braided hair in a lace dress that looked like it was from the 1930s. Her lips were as pink as the inside of a conch shell, her eyes sparkled with mischief. She guessed that this was Pearl, before she passed on, and she was gorgeous. Iris told herself that the delicate quivering excitement she felt was because of Pearl's current state. Of course, she was bewitching. She was a ghost. Iris felt sure that if a boy ghost shared these things with her, she would feel the exactly same way. She was reasonably sure of this.

Bastien said, "How long have you been in contact with Pearl?"

"Just under two months. I want it to stop. And I kind of don't want it to stop at the same time. I mean, Pearl is sweet, most of the time. But sometimes she gets…. Needy."

Bastien cupped his chin in his hand. He was such a beautiful man, almost as pretty as a girl. Iris snipped that thought as soon as it sprang up. Thoughts like that, thoughts about Pearl were poisonous weeds. The sickly kind that emerged from cracks in the concrete.

He said, "The idea of a 'hungry ghost' is a concept in Buddhist thought. It's probably older than the religion itself. A Hungry Ghost is a spirit that is entranced with the world of the living.

They long for warmth and light, the scents and sensations of living. Spirits that hover around people often become jealous of those of us that live. They can become parasitic, even if they don't mean to."

'Hungry ghost' was a perfect description of what Pearl had become. She took up more and more space in her brain. Pearl visited her at night, a roiling pink woman-shaped cloud. She would see the shape of color fluctuating at the foot of her bed, waiting. At first, it was just the 'conversations,' the pummeling images that left no space for her own. Then, somehow, Pearl entered her dreams. Iris would wake up groggy, the wisps of dream swirling around her head. She knew that they were Pearl's thoughts. She saw the bizarre architecture of shell-like buildings, their curves and bumps and spirals. She saw women, both white and black, nude, starred with sand, some of them with webbed fingers and the scaled tails of fish. These women and mermaids were always caught in some private ecstasy, their eyes slitted as their hands roamed over their bodies, pausing at their engorged breasts, and the mounds of their sex. Iris was intrigued, even aroused by the display of female flesh. But was the arousal her own, or Pearl's? She couldn't tell anymore. For now, the disturbing images only haunted her sleep. How long before she began hallucinating in the daytime?

She said, "How do I get rid of her?"

Bastien stood up. "Wait here," he said. He left her alone in the aisle of gods. She felt their bead eyes on her skin, eager and questing. Iris turned around, and saw the statuette of a black mermaid staring at her. It stood about a foot high. Her scales were iridescent, and her hair was seaweed-green. Her skin was ebony, and her eyes were two chips of some blue stone that glittered. Her mouth was slightly open, sighing. She sat on a pedestal, with the words La Sirena carved in a flowing script.

Iris startled when Bastien returned. He had a small sachet of something in his hand, which he gave to her.

"Sprinkle this around your bed for two nights. That should be enough."

Iris hefted the sachet in her palm, felt the movement of granular things inside. "What is it?" she ask.

"Salt," he said. "Salt from the earth, not the sea. That will drive Pearl away."

Outside of Botánica Olokun, Iris opened the small bag of salt. The salt was rough-hewn crystalline pebbles. It was the color of La Sirena's skin.

14: XAVIER

He had spent four full days in the museum, from ten am to six pm, combing through the archives and the surplus holdings. Most of the time, he was the only museum visitor. A couple of groups of people had tramped through during his studies, but usually it was just Xavier, Lincoln and Dr. Lenski. Dr. Lenski was extremely helpful. But there was something off about him. He was always hovering around Xavier as he worked on his laptop. Xavier felt his eyes on him, as if Lenski was checking for something. He had a nervous energy that was jarring. But Xavier couldn't really complain. Lenski bought coffee and donuts in the morning, and even sent Linc out to get lunch every day he was there.

Going to the museum had been the right thing to do. In addition to what was hanging behind the glass, there was an extensive collection in storage. Xavier spent hours flipping through some of Whitby's earliest work. The museum had quite a few of her experiments, including her embroidery hoops and some handkerchiefs. There were also other paintings by Grayson, and the other artists as well. It was invaluable. It also felt…wrong. He thought back to the first time he'd seen a Whitby quilt. How it entranced him. The quilts, up close, were so much less. They were just rough bits of textile, clumsily stitched together. The colors didn't sing. They were just a bit of charming folk art, nothing more.

It was in stark contrast to the Tamar Dupré works. When he returned back to his rented room, Xavier would look at the collages. Those images seemed to be alive. The fuchsia moved, like an optical illusion. The flowers became a hidden face, or the body of a woman.

He asked Iris if he could show Dr. Lenski the rest of Dupré's work one evening over dinner.

"I don't think it's such a good idea," she said. "I mean, it is *her* artwork, after all. She didn't intend for it to be in a gallery."

"But I'm not asking for it to be put in a gallery. I just think the curator ought to see it."

She scowled at him. Xavier almost laughed out loud; the reaction was so disproportionate to the request. She was a strange lady, he thought, recalling the weird drunken conversation he'd had with her the other night.

Then Iris said, "When Tamar left Shimmer, she told me to burn the artwork. She said it represented a bad period in her life."

"I understand," he told Iris. He *still* intended to take some of the pictures to the museum. Iris, and for that matter, Tamar, would never know.

Xavier woke up early on the next day, went down to the basement, and took a couple of the Dupré pieces. They positively shivered with manic energy. He saw the face of the woman in the flower, the flower in the woman. The cut-up landscape of photographed water and plants moved beneath his eye. He carefully placed them flat in his briefcase, next to his laptop, and left.

He got to the museum early, but luckily, Linc was already there. He let him in.

"Howard's not here," he said to Xavier. There was something strange about his affect. His eyes were animated, and his breathing was rapid. Linc clasped Xavier's shoulders. There was excitement in his voice. It sounded like he could barely contain it. Xavier felt a wave of warmth wash over him, starting at his head, moving through his body, ending at his groin. It took a moment to recognize that the tremble he felt was desire. Linc was a bony scarecrow of a man. His clothes hung off his thin body like a billowing tent. His teeth were terrible, his face was gaunt and skeletal. But he had a handsome face, or least, one that would be handsome if it ever filled out. Linc, though, was a former methhead, Xavier was sure. He'd seen the signs. (Was Linc even off the drug?) The spark of desire died as quickly as it flared.

"Let me show you something," Linc said, and he tugged Xavier by one shoulder to the Grayson gallery.

Xavier was apprehensive. What could make Linc, who was usually calm, so agitated? Unkind thoughts and images of rose pipettes flashed through Xavier's head. Linc stopped tugging his arm when they reached the Grayson gallery. The lights were off.

"What did you want me to see?" he asked.

"Just watch the walls," Linc said.

There was nothing to see save the vague shapes of the hanging canvases. And then—

Light oozed from the hanging pictures. The orbs in Shadrach Grayson's paintings vibrated, pulsing out fuchsia light. Xavier had never been a fan of Grayson's work. It looked a little slapdash—lazy smears of dove and pearl grey for the sky, choppy blue for the waves, and the fuchsia suns were lopsided. But it was as if something had awoken them.

"You see it?" Linc asked.

"Yeah…" Xavier said, then stopped speaking because something new was happening. The glowing orbs were changing. Some of them sprouted the tubular bells of the marsh-bell. Other shapes emerged from the fiery purple.

"What is happening?" Xavier said after a while.

"You're the scholar," Linc said. "*You* tell me."

Xavier said nothing. There were no words for what was happening. The paintings were living things. Painting was both a verb and a noun and both aspects of that word were present. The daubs of grey clouds that moved, the white-capped blue water that undulated, the sun that was also a flower and a face. The motion of Grayson's paintings was mesmerizing. It was also unbalancing, in the way that many optical illusions were. Xavier looked away.

He said, "What about the other artwork?"

Xavier didn't wait for an answer. He walked into the Descendants' gallery. Glass bottles winked like Christmas lights. The porcelain dolls' dresses looked like they were wreathed in purple flames. He left that gallery, entered into the main gallery. Whitby's quilts were also moving. They were still made of fabric, but it moved like water, like grass in the wind. And the marsh-bells became women, became one woman.

Xavier said, "When did this start?"

Linc had a grin on his face, a look of child-like wonder. "I noticed it about two weeks ago," he said. "Howard left for a doctor's appointment. *Then* the artwork came alive. It's miraculous. Like crying statues, or seeing Jesus in your toast. I tried to take pictures of it. But they never come out right. They're all blurred and weird."

The whole gallery was haywire, a riotous spectacle of flashing color. It was just like when he first saw the Whitby tapestry years ago, that same thrill. Xavier felt a bubble of wild joy grow in his chest. It grew and grew, transparent and iridescent, until it was the size of his heart. What would happen if it burst?

Linc continued, breathless with excitement. "When I first came on, Howard told me that the custodian before me, a dude named Gerald, quit because the museum was haunted. I thought nothing of it. People can be crazy, right? Then, when Howard left, stuff started happening. I stayed late that night, trying to capture it. Of course, it failed.

"I came in the next morning, and everything was still. It took me a couple of times to put it together. *She* doesn't show herself to Howard. Or, to just anyone. She only reveals herself to *certain* people."

Xavier was going to ask Linc about Howard, specifically, in what way Dr. Lenski was a paranormal activity retardant, but there was a more pressing question: "Who is 'she'?"

"*She* is the ghost," Linc said. His tone suggested an unspoken *Obviously.*

"The ghost? You think Hazel Whitby is haunting the museum?" It sounded silly, to speak it aloud. To quantify the weirdness. And yet, there wasn't any other explanation.

"Maybe," Linc said. "I don't think she's trying to scare people, though."

He thought back to the Dupré collages he had in his briefcase. Why were they 'activated' if they weren't in the museum?

"Why did you think I would be able to see this?"

Linc said, "Because she told me."

They both heard the click of the front door lock, and turned to watch Howard Lenski enter the museum. As soon as he entered the room, the tapestries were just pieces of fabric. The nervous, euphoric energy became inert. It was sudden, and absolute. It was like when a cellphone conversation dropped, the words you just spoke snuffed out.

Dr. Lenski was oblivious. He said, "This time, I bought bagels, boys. Still carb-bombs, but I was getting tired of the sugar rush."

Both Linc and Xavier looked at each other. Xavier was certain that the two of them were telepathically thinking the same thing: *He did NOT just call us 'boys.'* It was unclear which one of them started it. Was it a smirk or a glint in the eye? Both of them began laughing, softly at first, but then it tumbled into guffaws.

"What's so funny?" Howard asked. He looked so confused, standing in the doorway with a paper bag of bagels in one hand. It was an effort not to laugh again.

"Inside joke," Linc said, and left presumably to start his rounds.

***

On the morning of the fourth day, Howard took Xavier to what was left of the Whitby mansion. Xavier wanted to take some pictures to include in his thesis.

"In the 1950s, a group of artists used the old Whitby house as a studio," Dr. Lenski said. They rode in his weathered boxy car on a road that had the bay on one side, and the marsh on the other. It was a clear day; the sky was blue, and sunlight spangled the waves. The marsh, on the right side, was dense with browning shrubs, dying vines and grasses. Xavier thought he saw a tent on one of the pieces of dry earth, camouflaged by old branches and bracken. Who would want to live in such a desolate and unforgiving place?

Dr. Lenski continued: "It was abandoned for a number of years before that. Then someone burned it down."

"They burned it down on purpose?"

The road they drove on was in bad repair. Xavier could feel every pothole and crack in the pavement. The bayside view ended, replaced by undeveloped, overgrown land. The Shimmer Marsh seemed to go on forever. A flock of long-necked, black-winged geese fluttered down into the marsh waters. Most of the plants were brown and dying, in preparation for winter. Xavier could have sworn that he saw a flash of bright purple among all the brown and grey.

"A gentleman by the name of Hosea Quarles was charged with arson and vandalism in 1959. At first, he said it was a mistake—a misplaced cigarette. But forensics found empty cans of gasoline nearby. He said that the place was cursed."

"Interesting." Of course, Xavier immediately thought about yesterday's weirdness. There was nothing demonic or sinister about it at all. In fact, it was quite the opposite. It was miraculous, even angelic. Xavier hadn't been raised religious. His folks were agnostic at best, and their decision not raise him in faith was a minor controversy with his grandparents. "Any particular reason why Hosea thought the Whitby house was cursed?"

"Well, he was a bit of an odd duck," Dr. Lenski continued. (Xavier thought, *Talk about the pot calling the kettle black.*) "Mr. Quarles, it turns out, was one of the artists in the loose collective that used the Whitby mansion as a makeshift studio. A group of artists—of all disciplines—had even rigged up a generator and installed a few electric lights in what used to be the dining room."

"What was his work like?"

"I've seen it. His daughter showed it to me when I took the position at the museum. She wanted to donate some of the artwork. The board, however, nixed the idea. They felt that given Quarles's history, it would be in poor taste. Anyway, he did a sort of calligraphy, using an imaginary script, mostly on pieces of butcher paper. He'd use anything he could get his hands on—watercolor, ink, even crayon. It's quite extraordinary, really. Paragraphs of the script, all, of course, in that spectrum between purple and pink. The script itself reminds me, a little, of Amharic. The geometry of the letters. But of course, it was just gobbledygook. Or, to be more academic about it, Asemtic Writing."

Xavier wanted to see the artwork. He needed to see the strange letters spill across the page. He knew that it was linked to all of the other artwork. And to the shimmering effulgences he'd seen yesterday.

"There must be more to the story."

The marsh finally ended in a small copse of trees in their autumn finery—russet, gold and crisped brown.

"Not really," said Dr. Lenski. "The house was technically a ruin anyway and had been considered an eyesore for years. No one was hurt. Shimmer at the time had a mostly African-American police force, so Hosea was only given a fine."

They turned onto a dirt road, at the end of which stood the quintessential haunted house. The sky was clear, the sunlight bright but the house itself exuded desolation. It was a three-story brick structure, a shell that had been scorched and partially reclaimed by the marsh. The windows were misshapen, no longer rectangular. The brick was no longer red. It was darkened and crumbling. Through the glassless windows, Xavier saw the rotted floors, where plants erupted. A mess of ferns and vines silently writhed in the interior. There were puddles of standing water, dark and still as voids.

"Jesus," said Xavier. "It's a little *Texas Chainsaw Massacre*, no?"

Dr. Lenski laughed, then said, "It's a mess. Just try to see past this ruin. Hazel Whitby made most of her work here."

Xavier took several pictures of the house with his camera phone. He thought about sending some shots to his professors, but decided against it. That would have been way too informal for them, especially Dr. Devine. He could see Dr. Giordano writing back with some deliciously arch caption, like 'Decrepit Homes and Gardens.' When he went to go inside, Dr. Lenski warned him to be careful.

"I'll just stay on the steps," Xavier replied. Though the steps were crumbling and not particularly safe. In fact, the whole structure should have been condemned.

The interior of the house was dark enough that he had to activate the flash option on his camera. He had a vague idea of what the images he captured were, but he would have to fix them in editing. The floor was alive, crawling with vegetation and, possibly, animals. The earthy smell of fungus and mold drifted up to tickle his nose. It was a good thing that he didn't go in. Xavier had a sudden feeling of vertigo, staring into that coiled darkness. He could see his body falling in, being ensnared by the vines, brushed by the tiny feet of insects, left to rot and enrich the soil. For one moment not longer than a blink, he *wanted* to be smothered by leaves and become one with the soil. *The marsh would love him, as it had all of the others. Maybe its murky waters would flow in his veins, and he'd start painting again.*

"Everything okay?" asked Dr. Lenski.

Xavier stepped away from the ruins, slightly dazed. "Yeah," he said. "I'm done."

15: FUCHSIA (1863)

Fuchsia stayed entwined with Hazel as she aged, until her fingers were sticks warped by arthritic pain. She was a vine that sprouted bright blossoms of color. She crawled and crept through the woman's soul like a snake. During that time, Hazel had children with Jethro; only three of them survived and each of the surviving ones was sold to settle some of the Whitbys' debts. For the most part, Fuchsia stayed out of Hazel's affairs. The work was what was important. The woman's life was just background chatter. Her pains, or for that matter, her joys meant little to Fuchsia. She felt, in an objectively distant way, the mix of terror and exhilaration when Jethro first fucked her. The blinding white pain of childbirth was nothing to the abyss Hazel descended into each time she lost a child to either death or the auction block. Each time, Fuchsia was banished to some dark cavern that sorrow hollowed out. Nothing could grow on that rocky ground, and the darkness swallowed all light, all color.

When her fifth child was sold at the age of three, and Hazel descended into a darkness that lasted months, Fuchsia knew that she had to do something. While she was in that darkness, bits and pieces of memory flashed. She remembered the chafing of shackles, the smallness of confinement, and yes, the yawning endlessness. Fuchsia never wanted to feel that way again.

***

"Can you put that down for a spell?" Jethro stood in the doorway of the attic.

Hazel stopped her needle, and glanced at him, avoiding his eyes.

When it was clear that she wasn't going to speak, Jethro said, "You been up here for three weeks. They understand that it's hard to lose a child. But that sympathy is running out."

"Do they," Hazel replied. "Do they really know what it's like to have their children sold like cotton, or a barrel of sorghum?"

"I suppose not," he said, not unkindly. "Still. They *own* you. You're their servant. They're talking. Master thinks that you've gone mad, even says that he shoulda sold you along with Linus."

"Let them," she said, turning back to the quilt she was working on.

"You shouldn't say that," Jethro whispered. "They might sell you to someone who will work you to death."

What was death, compared to living in a world where your own flesh and blood could be taken away from you at a moment's notice? The other slaves constantly told her how nice the Whitbys were, that they were saints compared to the Buchanans down the road who chopped off fingers and toes of disobedient slaves, or the Millers, who had an abnormally large number of mulattoes working their tobacco fields. Working for the Whitbys was a cakewalk, compared to working in the fields. Hazel no longer believed that was true, if she ever did. She realized that she could work her fingers to bloody stumps and still be considered no more important than a mule.

She went back to sewing, ended the conversation.

A few days later, she was called down to meet with Helena Whitby in the parlor. The Missus had a stern look on her face.

"Hazel," she began, crossing her arms, "I remember when you were an industrious, faithful worker."

Hazel glanced down, a suitable posture for chastisement.

"Can you be that girl again?" said the Missus.

It was that word. *Girl*. She'd been with child more than Helena Whitby had, and had those kids taken away. But she was still a *girl*. She was almost thirty years of age, but she was still a girl. Less than a girl. But she was a Negro, and her lot in life was to suffer. Still, the word Girl bothered her, like sand grit in her shoe, or a canker sore. She knew that she should take the admonishment with servile, Christian humility. But she hated Helena Whitby, with her sour milk complexion and her pettiness. She, and her dour, drunken husband had made Jethro her husband, had taken Sally, Myrtle and Linus away from her. Master Whitby spent all of his money on liquor. She'd seen his cold rages first hand. And his wife, beribboned and corseted like a fat doll, loved her laudanum. Those two were the reason Hazel heard her children's voices, disturbing her sleep. Why she could no longer bear to lay beneath Jethro.

"You done took my children away," Hazel found herself saying, "and you just worried about dust in your bedroom."

Mrs. Whitby scowled at her. "I will *not* tolerate such insolent sassing from a servant. I demand an apology."

"I am sorry," Hazel said, "that you took my babies."

Helena Whitby's face quivered like a jelly. Her cheeks reddened to the color of cranberries. Her already thin lips became a tight line. It was almost comic, watching her eyes glaze over with rage.

"You black devil!" she sputtered out. Then she boxed Hazel's ears.

Her ears rang and rang and rang. Her brain was jostled, blood and bone vibrated. It was a wrong sort of feeling, that something vital had shattered. It was worse than hitting a funny bone, slightly better than a bitten tongue. Hazel's balance shifted—

(And Fuchsia woke. In between the tintinnabulation in Hazel's head. Between the waves and pain. Fuchsia did not just wake. She reacted. She darted, like a bird, right out of Hazel, and into Helena.

Helena's soul was an alien place, full of jarring, laudanum-tinged whispers. It was porridge-bland, grey and beige and as ordered as a linen closet. There was no warmth in there, no color. And she, Fuchsia, was color itself. A wave of light, between purple and pink. Vibrant and vivid. She hated this place, the pasty pale glob of malice and uniformity. And it hated her back, her blackness, her pinkness, her purpleness. Fuchsia screamed in that airless, loveless, colorless place. A scream of rage, a scream that stained the pristine starched whiteness.

Then Fuchsia fled, back into the bustling familiarity of Hazel.)

Helena Whitby had a stunned look on her face, as if *her* ears had been boxed. The pink drained out of her face as she stepped away from Hazel.

"What did you do to me?" she asked.

"You're the one who hit me," Hazel replied.

"There's something in my head," Mrs. Whitby continued as if she didn't hear Hazel. "Help me lay down."

Hazel led the woman to the powder blue fainting couch. Mrs. Whitby rested her head against the raised edge. She lay still for a while.

"You'll have to fetch my medicine," she said.

Hazel got the tincture, along with a tiny silver teaspoon. Mrs. Whitby raised her beribboned head and opened her eyes in order to take the medicine.

She screeched. "I still see it, in front of me!" Mrs. Whitby shut her eyes.

"See what?" Hazel asked.

"Shapes. Lines. Wavy lines that glow. The lines are the same horrid color as your quilts."

Hazel set the tincture bottle and spoon on a side table. She sat on the couch next to her mistress, not knowing why. Her movements weren't her own, like when worked on the quilts. When this happened, Hazel felt a gentle bliss. Bliss as soft as silk, as beautiful as a storm of petals. She placed her hands on Mrs. Whitby's sweating forehead.

"What are you doing?"

"Shhh," said Fuchsia.

She rubbed Helena Whitby's temples, in a circular pattern. The woman moaned beneath her ministrations, feeling the bolt of pain as it moved through her head, through her skin. Hazel stopped rubbing. There it was, a thin thread of fuchsia. She slowly pulled it out of the woman's head, winding it around her finger. When she finished, Mrs. Whitby was asleep.

"Remember," she whispered to the resting white woman, "I can always put it back."

16: LINCOLN

The soul is soil, she said.

She told him in last night's dream. Had spoken the words, even pointed to the ground beneath her feet. When Linc looked down, he saw that she had no feet. Two legs just grew up from the muddy earth. At the time, it made sense. Of course. She was the marsh-bell, or the spirit of the marsh-bell. Her filmy gown had once been petals, probably still *were* petals in some sense. He remembered her words, the urgency and the wisdom of them, but he could not recall her voice. Had she even moved her lips?

Soil is the soul. Was his soul like the earth, dark and seething with roots and worms? No. His soul was tainted, littered with broken glass and chemical poison. Things died in him. He was a freak with rotting teeth, heroin-thin and a rootless drifter. If he was earth, he was salted earth, incapable of harboring life.

Then she handed him something. It was a pod of some kind, about the size of an egg. It was green, bifurcated with brownish seams.

He held it in his cupped palm. It burst open, and maybe one hundred seeds fell out. The seeds looked like feathers, like dandelion fluff. Like mist given shape and form.

"You're not real," he said. His voice was loud and out of place in this place of blue skies, rippling grass and marbled waters.

She laughed, in that soundless way. Her face was plain. She was even a little chubby and her skin tone was uneven, darker brown around her eyes, and her neck. Her hair was styled in plaits that spidered out from her head. She could have been some distant cousin, or a girl seen on the streets of DC.

"Are you Hazel?" he said, in his too-loud boombox of a voice.

She shook her head. *No.*

"Then who are you?"

She didn't reply. She just pointed to the seed pod. Even now, they were scattering across the marsh, settling on the water and the few spots of dry land.

The soul is the soil!

***

Every night was like that, the day after the artwork came alive. His dreams were technicolor and psychedelic, full of purple flowers that became people, all in the same shimmering marsh. He would walk in the marsh, come across a flowering marsh-bell. He might pluck one of them, and they would become a person, dressed in fuchsia clothing. The men might wear trousers or overalls or some-times, robes. One man wore a full three-piece suit. The women sometimes wore pants, but for the most part were garbed in flow-ing gowns. One woman wore an ornate church hat. There were at least two of the flower people whose genders he couldn't determine. It didn't matter, though. Only their art. Each one of the marsh-bell people started painting, or sewing or illustrating. One person made tarot cards, all of them with a marsh-themed background. All of the Major Arcana wore purple raiments. Another person dressed porcelain dolls in glowing outfits.

Linc knew that these were the acolytes of the marsh spirit. She was their muse. And now, he was invited to join them.

As he learned the stories of the acolytes, Linc noticed certain patterns, ones besides the obvious flower/woman/color motif. Mainly, that each acolyte created their icons alone. The art was private, an esoteric mystery, just made for her and her acolytes. It did not belong in a gallery, for public consumption, because it was sacred. The art was a portal to her, and her realm. The museum did not need to exist, but now that it did, it was a kind of temple. It was a hidden temple, though. Hidden in plain sight, because she only revealed herself to certain people. Blessed ones.

For the first time in his life, Linc was chosen, was blessed. The freakishly tall one who wasn't good at basketball like he should have been. The son who wasn't as talented as his older sister. The one too bougie to fit in with Violet Rage. The one time he tried to fit in, he'd gotten addicted and thrown out of his house. But now, he belonged to a secret society. He had never been religious, never understood that kind of connection. But now, he was connected to her.

Her. What was her name? Maybe she didn't have a name. She just was. Maybe she would reveal her name eventually. In the meantime, he had to make his own portal to her, somehow.

***

It was one in the morning when he left his motel room. He had seen the light, spilling between the seam in the blackout curtains. At first, he thought it was light from the motel's neon sign. A couple of weeks ago, the A in Bayside sputtered and strobed before it gave up the ghost. But the sign's light was as red as an apple. This light was different. When he parted the curtain, he saw a ball of light, the color of a marsh-bell, hovering outside of his window. It was like one of Shadrach Grayson's orbs had become detached from its painting.

There was a chill in the air, but that just invigorated him. He walked along a path on the side of the road that closely followed the salt marsh. Linc had no destination in mind. The orb was roughly circular, full of movement, pellucid filmy veils of pink-purple flames, like a tiny sun. Linc knew that this was no hallucination or trick of the light. It was an invitation. A calling.

He dressed quickly, taking up his backpack, and left the room. The will-o'-the-wisp was already across the parking lot, patiently waiting for him.

He followed it. It moved down the empty road, pausing every now and then, waiting for him to catch up.

The first time Lincoln did meth, it felt like his nerves had been plucked like the strings of a harp. A wave of glorious sound washed down his body from his brain down to his toes. The world slowed down to a crawl and he was moving at the speed of sound. His nerves were made of diamond and every thought, every motion vibrated with crystallized energy. He understood why it was called crystal meth. When he was on it, he was a being created of strands of some impervious substance.

But, meth often came bundled with anxiety: the crystal harp was too tightly strung. Plucking the strings drew blood, changing the tone. And then, there was the come down, an untuned harp playing songs of rage and paranoia.

Now, he felt the same way. No, he felt *better* than then. There was no anxiety, only wild, unfettered joy. Every atom of his being was filled with this emotion. This was real, and not synthetic emotion.

He walked for a while. Maybe miles. He wasn't sure, and he didn't check the time. The immensity of the Shimmer Marsh spread out on his left side. Even in autumn, Linc could feel the life surging in the waters, in the grasses. Things swam, or slithered or flew there. The smell of salt and algae was pungent. Just a thin ribbon of tarmac held it back, barely containing the wet wilderness. Not even the lights lining the road could penetrate the darkness. But that was okay. Linc could see, now. Every blade and every ripple. He heard every whisper of wind, every bird cry.

On and on the orb went, around bends in the road.

I could follow her forever, he thought.

And, just as he thought that, the orb stopped.

There was a cement building, covered in vines. It was once white, but the paint peeled off. It was probably an old garage. There were rust stains in the shape of long-removed signs. What windows had been there were long gone.

The will-o'-the-wisp fluttered against the wall that was most free of vines, and then smashed itself against the wall. It vanished.

Linc laid down his backpack, and pulled out a can of red spray paint. It was the wrong color, of course. But that didn't matter. He had no particular skill, and that didn't matter either.

She would guide him.

17: FUCHSIA (1870)

They told him, *There's haints in that house.*

The house was in good, if not pristine, condition. Shadrach heard that it had been abandoned a couple of years ago, that the family had lost money after the war and had moved to a major city, in search of steady work. It was a large house that faced the saltwater marsh. Three-story, red brick with a wide wooden porch. It still had intact windows, and the yard, while overgrown, wasn't yet wild. He'd seen, and slept in, burnt out houses. Places where the floors were rotted through and rain fell from the roof. Places where wildlife nested. Once, he had shared a house with an ornery weasel and her pups. Furthermore, haunting wasn't necessarily a deterrent. He stayed in a supposedly haunted house with a bunch of other fellow drifters somewhere in Pennsylvania. The "haunting" consisted of a couple creaks and what sounded like footsteps. Shadrach was the only one who had stayed through the night. In the morning, he'd found a nest of decidedly unghostlike raccoons.

***

After the war, the world was full of haunted houses. He'd traveled with a carnival, as a part of the Gallery of Human Oddities and

Curiosities up and down the East Coast for three years, passing through towns still damaged. North of the Mason-Dixon line, the crowds were mainly composed of women bereft of husbands and sons. South, there were entire ghost towns full of burned and abandoned buildings. Everyone, Negro or white, had the same bleak, hard-bitten look. Only children were immune to this mood, as pervasive as an illness.

Kids were the best audience, eager to see Magda the Werewolf Woman, Petra the Pinhead or even himself: Shad the Spotted Negro. Their faces lit up with wild, untrammeled joy or horror when members of the troupe walked on stage. Sometimes, their laughter would encourage a smile or two from the adults.

It was that innocent joy that got him into the traveling carnival business in the first place. He'd been a worker at a textile factory in Ohio then, toiling over the dye vats, immersed in chemical fumes, stained with a rainbow of dyes. People tended to notice that, instead of the skin condition, and for a while, that was a blessing. He had been fourteen when the first patch showed up on the back of his hand. He had worn gloves to cover the patch, which looked like someone had grafted a white man's skin there. When Shadrach turned sixteen, the splotch had grown and was joined by pale pink circles around his eyes. By that time, he had given up wearing gloves and dealt with endless stares, awkward questions and overheard insults. *Was it leprosy? That man looks like an appaloosa. Is it contagious? He looks like a reverse raccoon.* When Cecil Barrett asked him to join the show a few years later, the prospect of entertaining people, especially kids, was appealing. It was much better than the exhausting shifts at the factory. Besides, he would get to travel.

The work was easy. Shadrach had no extra talent. He was, instead, a living statue with a rapidly developing deformity. He just sat on a stool in a wagon that had been transformed into a kind of stage and let people gawp at him. The adults murmured among themselves, cruel and curious things he was, by now, thoroughly used to. *I think it's paint. It's like he's molting—like a snake! That's the ugliest nigger I ever seen.* The children, however, were guileless. There was no spite in their observations. He saw wonder and terror on their little faces.

Also, he was not the only one they came to stare at. Hirsute Magda, or gentle Petra were more popular attractions. The small group went from Ohio to Pennsylvania and then to New Jersey, mostly visiting small towns, though sometimes they would set up on the outskirts of large cities. Sometimes Mr. Barrett would come across other human oddities and added them to his show. That's how he met Luigi.

Luigi was a dwarf, standing just under five feet tall. He was well-muscled and had many tattoos beneath his dusky olive skin. He had curly black hair and piercing black eyes beneath his prominent brow. He joined the troupe somewhere in New Jersey, south of New York City. In addition to being the resident little person (he was dubbed "WeeGee"), he could also juggle. Pins, balls, and knives. (He tried to juggle flaming hoops, but he did not succeed.) Luigi and Shadrach became fast friends, sharing meals, moonshine, cigars, and, eventually, their bodies with each other. When Mr. Barrett caught wind of the buggery, both them were kicked out of the troupe. Luigi returned to New Jersey, and the troupe left Shadrach behind in the small Eastern Shore town where the last show had been.

***

Shimmer was a strange little town, in a limbo area between Maryland and Delaware. The marsh wrapped around the town, making it prone to flooding and bad for farming. A community of colored watermen eked out a living in this harsh environment, harvesting and selling crabs and oysters to more affluent areas. They were a clannish, taciturn bunch. None of the adults cracked a smile at the show and some of the overheard chatter wasn't that flattering. *I already know a dwarf,* one woman mumbled. Someone else claimed to have known other Negroes with his skin condition. In spite of this apparent familiarity with 'freaks,' no one would rent a room to him.

So here he was, on the outskirts of town, looking for a way into a haunted house. Except, of course, it wasn't haunted. It was just abandoned. From what Shadrach could glean, in addition to the money troubles, the Whitbys moved because of the mistress's ill health. Something about a nervous condition, one that made her see things that weren't there. He suspected that this was the germ of the ghost rumor. Even if there were a haint or two, surely he would not be the target of their ire. It/they would just probably ignore him, like most of the living did anyway.

Shadrach found some unlocked cellar doors at the back of the house. Opening them released a gust of dank, stale air. It was dark down there, and he could see that there had been some minor flooding. He kept the cellar doors open for the sunlight and walked down the stairs. He walked through several large puddles. The unfinished floor was slippery with mud that made a squelching sound with every step he took. He wiped his boots on the first stair that ostensibly led up to the house.

Behind the door at the top of the stairs was a bare room, the wooden floor coated in furry dust. He saw the impressions of furniture shapes. There was where the couch was. Here, the trapezoidal shape of a pianoforte. The house was utterly empty, as he had expected. Entering each room set off a flurry of dust. He traversed the entirety of the house, looking for a suitable place to sleep. Shadrach intended to stay only one night, and then leave this Godforsaken waterlogged place.

On the second floor, he found that the last room at the end of the hall, presumably the master bedroom, had one piece of furniture. An armoire. It loomed in the corner of the room on its wooden paws. It was a three-paneled monstrosity, one that was firmly shut. It was in pristine condition, with warm walnut paneling, and looked like it had just been varnished. Why did it disturb him? He'd seen abandoned furniture before, perfectly usable canopy beds and chests. Then, in the waning light, Shadrach saw what was wrong with the armoire. There wasn't a speck of dust on the thing. The rest of the rooms were filled with dust. And yet, somehow, this lone piece was speck-free, and shone with a dark luster.

It's just an armoire, he told himself. Maybe someone had been in the house recently, someone who impulsively cleaned the wood. That, of course, was ridiculous.

I'll bet that it's not as nice as it seems. The inside is probably rotted or stained somehow.

He opened one of the panels, the middle one.

It was a fairly wide space, perhaps the size of a ten-year-old child in height, and the width of a shoulder. The space was filled to the top with linen. Shadrach thought, *At least I'll have something to sleep on other than the wooden floor.* He pulled out a piece, laid it on the floor. It was a tapestry of some kind, one with clashing colors and shapes that didn't make any sense. Splotches of blue, brown and purple were arranged in childlike blobs full of clumsy stitching. Shadrach did not particularly care for the blanket's pattern. It managed to be both deliberate and wild. No wonder these pieces were abandoned along with the armoire. The loud colors and strange shapes were disturbing to look at, because he could almost perceive an order to the thing. Was the blue a river, or lake? The brown, earth? And was that purple blob a flower or a person? In the end, it did not matter. Shadrach pulled out a few more of the folded blankets, and found that they were variations on the same theme, as if their creator were obsessively perfecting their work.

Seven or so quilts made Shadrach's makeshift bed. They were in immaculate condition, as if they had been laundered the day they had been entombed.

***

When Hazel died, Fuchsia tumbled in darkness. She saw Hazel's soul leave, a tremulous pearl-shaped thing that floated up, up, up into the endlessly roiling sky of black clouds. Fuchsia, however, fell. Drifted downwards, also pearl-shaped but not the starry white of Hazel's soul. She was the wrong color. Hazel went up to the sky beyond the clouds. Fuchsia sank down into the soil, like a seed.

And there she waited, a weak light against the loam that surrounded her. Did she sleep? Maybe. She forgot her name, shed her color for a while.

Things came back to her, stirred her in her grave. They did not make sense, but they were comforting, just the same. She remembered sunsets in the marsh, the way the sun melted into the water, the way the water drank the sun until its light spilled across the surface. She remembered the sound of frogs and birds as they echoed across the marsh. The insects that looked like glittering jewels as they flew among the grasses. And the moon on clear nights, a bright coin of silver.

I had a name, she thought. It was buried. Deep, deep. Like she was buried, now.

I have a new name.

The soil could no longer contain Fuchsia. She grew, like a plant. Up through the layers of dirt, through water, through topsoil.

***

Shadrach awoke in the misty grey predawn. He was refreshed. It had been ages since he'd had a good sleep. After being kicked out of the carnival, he'd slept in barns, on the bare earth, on beaches, and beneath the porch ceilings of abandoned houses. His nights were interrupted by mosquitoes, stray dogs, and, a few times, by armed and angry white men. There were days where he stumbled through, exhausted. Sleeping on the nest of quilts had been a great idea. He thought he might stay around for a while.

Shadrach went to the town later that day, picking up dry goods and some lamp oil with the few coins he had left over. People stared at him with suspicion. Nothing that he wasn't used to. He was a pariah. He might as well live in a pariah house. Back in the cellar, there had been a couple of abandoned kerosene lamps, and a few battered pots. These were probably meant to be used by the servants. He cooked his meal outside, a thick gruel of cornmeal sprinkled with some salt pork, facing the marsh, over a small fire. There was a fire pit that was probably used to boil water for laundry and bath water, and a working well.

He stayed in the house for a week. The days were filled with him looking for odd jobs in the town. At the carnival, in addition to being an attraction, he was a handyman. By the end of the week, widows and women whose husbands were watermen asked him to fix broken stairs, carry groceries, and mend broken fences. It was satisfying work. He wandered back to the house at the edge of the marsh just as evening fell. He would eat a quick supper, which the women often sent home with him in a covered basket, and fall asleep on the quilts.

Over time Shadrach pulled all of the quilts from the armoire. He laid them down on the floor, and pinned up the ones he found particularly interesting on the wall. He hung them on the stair banisters, draped them in window alcoves. Soon, the top floor was covered with the quilts. Fully spread out, the quilts formed a kind of landscape map. They described the topography of a marsh, the idealized version of the one surrounding Shimmer. He would still sleep on several of them as a makeshift bed. He had never slept so well.

***

Birdie Vogt was a handsome woman, light-skinned and freckled, with a reddish tinge to her hair. Ever since she had been widowed, single men hovered around her like they were bees and she was a nectar-full flower in bloom. They bought her flowers and sweets, hoping to woo her. When that failed, they took her ten-year-old son Cephas out fishing or offered to apprentice him to one trade or another. But Cephas, like his mother, was distant and as nonreactive as a rock. She claimed to be waiting for her husband, missing for four years and most likely dead. Shadrach thought that she just wanted to be alone, that she was tired of being married. Some folks liked to be alone, like himself.

When he went to her small homestead to deliver goods from the general store, he overheard people talking about her.

The men would say things like, *It's a damn shame that a woman that fine is frigid!*

The women would say, *Poor thing, she ain't been right since Ira run off!*

Miss Birdie was not talkative during his visits. She'd often sit on the porch knitting or sipping coffee, and watch him as he worked. She was a gentle, comforting presence. That suited him just fine. She allowed him to teach Cephas how to paint, to mend a fence, to drive a horse and wagon, and how to fish. In return, she let him stay for dinner some evenings.

The Vogts were a reticent bunch, and the meal would often pass with nary a word spoken.

One evening, Miss Birdie called Cephas and Shadrach to dinner. The days had gotten shorter by then, and the sun set around five, so dinner was earlier.

"Word around town is that you're squatting over at the Whitby place," she said after the grace was said. "People seen you walking from that direction."

Shadrach nodded. "Ain't nobody living there," he said. "It's as good a place as any to stay."

"That place is haunted!" said Cephas. His eyes sparkled with excitement.

"Hush, child," Miss Birdie said.

"I haven't seen any haints. But if I do, I'll be sure to tell you about it." Shadrach winked at Cephas.

"Don't encourage him," Miss Birdie said. "I used to know the folks that lived in that house. The colored folk, anyway. My mother was friends with the housemaid, Judith. They would meet each other in town when they were doing errands. The stories she would tell about that family!"

"What stories?" Cephas asked.

"Stop playing with your food, child," Miss Birdie said. "Well, Mr. Whitby liked his liquor, and he had a reputation for being a mean drunk. He was a lawyer, and he lost quite a few clients. Judith also said that his wife was a nervous wreck. The two sons were like night and day. The older one went to Harvard, up north, and he never came back. And the younger one was a drunk, like his daddy. The younger one racked up a bunch of gambling debts. He was terrible at cards and dice. His daddy had to pay off Junior's debts many a time."

"Get to the ghost part!" said Cephas.

"I don't know if there's a ghost in this story or not. But there's a whole lot of strangeness. Judith worked alongside some mighty strange Negroes. Caleb, the house steward, had once been a freeman. He never told Judith how he ended up being the Whitby's slave."

Shadrach said, "I heard that some white folks would get a free nigger high on morphine, slipping it in his drink after being all friendly-like. When the nigger wakes up, he'd be in the South, on some auction block somewhere."

Cephas gasped, his eyes as wide as saucers.

"Well Caleb wasn't just any freedman," Miss Birdie continued. "He was an educated one. He knew a couple of languages. Even a few dead ones."

"How can a language die?" said Cephas. "Are they even alive?"

Miss Birdie ignored her son. "Then there was the other maid. Hazel. She was younger than Judith. They had bought her when she was a child. She was a little touched, even then. My daddy was a white man who had taken my mother as a wife. We were 'owned' by him in law, but we was more or less free. I remember Daddy taking me to the Whitby house for some reason or other. It doesn't matter. But I met Hazel a couple of times. I remember one time in particular. She was maybe in her twenties, and pregnant. Daddy had her watch over me while he conducted his business with Mr. Whitby.

"I remember that she took me to a small sewing room, filled with scraps of fabric and various tools, like scissors, awls and needles. It smelled nice, like bergamot tea. She gave me a cookie or a biscuit, then sat down, and began working on a quilt.

"I was ten or so at the time. Daddy and Mamma told me I was seeing things, but I swear I saw this: Hazel threaded a needle and started sewing—with her eyes closed. It was like she was asleep, but every movement was precise. The work was delicate, but her needle didn't snag. She didn't prick herself, not once. And, the whole time, she *smiled*."

"This Hazel," Shadrach said, "she probably sewed a lot of things."

"Obsessively," said Miss Birdie. "She was—the word that Judith used was *driven*. Like she couldn't control it. 'Something's moving through her,' I heard Judith say. I'll never forget that smile. I've seen that look before. In church, when people get the Spirit inside of them…"

"What did Hazel look like?" Shadrach asked, after a long pause. Miss Birdie's attention had drifted. Her eyes pointed toward the china hutch, but he knew that she didn't see it.

"Hazel was pretty enough," said Miss Birdie, "short, a little plump, dark brown skin. Her children were all sold, to pay for the son's gambling debts.

"That's where the real strange part of the story comes in."

Cephas's eyes glittered with excitement.

"Around the time the fourth child had been sold, Helena Whitby, the mistress, began having headaches. Real bad ones, the type where you see images. She told Mamma that the Missus became addicted to morphine. Judith said that she became a drooling mess. What a nightmare it must have been: living with a drunk, a drug-addled woman, and a scoundrel son. Well, Hazel got scarlet fever that winter and died shortly after. Mrs. Whitby's headaches increased. She began to complain of bright lines of color in her vision, and dizziness. She claimed that it was because all of those quilts Hazel made were somehow connected to her headaches. Something about the colors Hazel used."

"So, Hazel haunted the Whitbys, and drove 'em out of town!" said Cephas. He was beside himself with the macabre story.

"That was the rumor around town," said Miss Birdie. "You ain't seen nothing strange at the house, have you, Mr. Grayson?"

***

It was hard to get used to the rhythms of Shadrach's mind. It was completely unlike Hazel's. Where Hazel's thoughts had been as quick as hares in the underbrush, Shadrach's mind was slow and becalmed, like a turtle on land. He was a man who gave himself to muscle memory. As he worked, he never lost himself in thought. He was always in the here-and-now, present, thoroughly aware of his surroundings. Each thought was deliberate, a finely crafted, solid thing, not like the lacy, wispy train of Hazel's mind. Fuchsia thought that this was due to his maleness.

He had had a hard life, one that did not allow for flights of fancy. He was permanently in survival mode. Shadrach's body was always ready to flee or face threats. He kept his emotions blunted.

The topsoil of Shadrach's psyche was thin and rocky. It was difficult to find purchase there. So Fuchsia went deep, to the sleeping side of his soul, where the ground was moist and rich. Shadrach's dreams were chaotic and joyless things. It was like a storm. In between the gusts, she saw that Shadrach had lived a life dictated by grim circumstance, devoid of any beauty.

She was just a seed, floating on gale-force winds.

***

This house is not haunted.

Shadrach told himself that. And he believed it, for the most part. It was easy to ignore that the quilts he slept on and the ones he hung up never seemed to get dirty. Also, there seemed to be a never-ending supply of them. The armoire was a bottomless coffin. When did Hazel ever get any actual work done? He counted at least one hundred of them before he stopped. But there always seemed to be more stuffed in the cavity. He was forever unfolding them.

Shadrach hadn't remembered his dreams since he was a teenager, when he had an embarrassing wet dream full of shirtless boys bathing in the creek behind his parents' house. It wasn't something that bothered him. But in this not-haunted house, he dreamed each and every night. They were rich and luminous dreams, full of tranquility. He looked forward to sleeping, for the first time in a long while. The colors were vibrant, intense. All of them were in the marsh, a marsh where the water was clear as crystal. Where brightly colored fish swam, and blue herons stalked them. Where the grass was soft as carpet, and insects hung in the air like jewels. Where it was always the moment before twilight starts, and the sky is indigo, and the sun just begins to turn orange. These dreams were not hauntings, though. They were just dreams.

Shadrach was never alone in this dream-marsh. She was always off in the distance, at the horizon's edge or on one of the islets, gazing in the distance. She never looked at him directly, but she clearly knew Shadrach was there. They might spend the entire dream on different islets, sharing silence. Sometimes, she wasn't a young woman, wrapped in purple. Instead, she was just a flower, one the same color as her robes. And sometimes, she was a formless, glowing shape, a bright ball of light hovering above the waters.

But this was not a haunting. It was just Miss Birdie's crazy stories, and the townsfolks' superstition rattling around in his brain.

***

What am I doing? Shadrach thought. It was night and the sky was starless and mist leaked from the Shimmer Marsh as thick as clouds. He was outside, like a fool, because he had seen something. Or rather, he *thought* he had seen something.

He pushed through brush at the marsh's edge. There was much crackling in the undergrowth, both his own and other unseen creatures'. He had seen hares and foxes, and the occasional deer during his stay in the Whitby house. They were probably confused as to why he was out on a misty night like this. He didn't even have a lantern.

Shadrach had woken up early, startled into the predawn darkness by something that had spilled over from a dream. The dream was not a nightmare. It was, in fact, a wonderful dream, one that he wished would never end. He and the woman in purple were finally on the same islet, watching as the sun sank down into the water. They stood side by side in silence for a while. Then he turned to face her. Her face was round, her brown eyes sparkled. Her hair was plaited and woven with flowers. Her robe-like dress fluttered, even though there was no breeze. She moved toward him, her mouth shaping words he couldn't hear.

Your name, he said, *what's your name?*

She replied, "…"

And he woke up, grasping for a sound.

Her face faded from the air. It was replaced by a glowing sphere the same color as her fluctuating dress. The tiny purple sun hovered in front of his face before leaving the room. He chased after it, straight into the misty woods.

The orb led him to the edge of the Shimmer Marsh, and vanished when he arrived. The marsh was alive in the darkness, full of frog and bird song. The grasses shivered in the wind.

Shadrach searched the shore for the little light.

"Don't leave me now," he said to the marsh. "I know you are real." He felt like a fool. *It's just a delusion,* he thought, *crazy stories that made my imagination go haywire.* In spite of this, he felt that someone was listening. The air grew still, and the sounds of the marsh paused.

Shadrach asked, "What is your name?"

His voice was absorbed by the marsh.

A minute passed in silence.

And then, she answered.

18: IRIS (2010)

Shimmer was as thick with ghosts as it was with fog and seagulls. Iris saw them clustering around the immensity of the marsh when she drove home from work. They were like thermal signatures, blotches of color with random features visible, like a hand or half of a face. For the most part, they ignored her as assiduously she ignored them.

Other than the ghosts, Iris loved the coastal town. She had thought she was a city girl to her core, but it turned out not to be true. The slower pace of things suited her well. When Tamar and she moved to Shimmer, Iris expected to be bored. Adjusting to Shimmer's gentle rhythms had been difficult the first year. Tamar's dad made it plain from jump that he thought their 'lifestyle' was sinful, and while he and his daughter eventually came to an understanding, it was clear that Iris was still persona non grata. The townsfolk themselves were a reserved bunch, suspicious of outsiders. Most of them had roots in the town since before the Civil War. The townsfolk had a curious mixture of Northern stoicism and Southern hospitality. But gradually, people warmed to their presence. They came to be known as, alternately, as 'Ernest's Girls,' and Tamaris. When Ernie died, the townsfolk came out to his funeral and the house was filled with cakes and casseroles for weeks. Shimmer became home.

***

"How do I look?" Tamar walked into the room in a silk peach dress and matching slingbacks. As always, her hair had a flower pinned in it, a pink hibiscus. She smelled of orange blossoms and sandalwood, and her neck was encircled by a black bead necklace.

"Stunning, as always." Iris wore a simple black crepe smock accented with a rose quartz necklace. Other than a touch of lipstick, she didn't bother with makeup. Tamar had a layer of foundation and faint hints of blush along her cheeks.

"I hope there will be food," said Tamar. She gathered up a matching clutch and began transferring some items from her bigger purse.

"I'm sure that there will be some. At least cheese and crackers. Maybe wine."

"Well, I'm hoping for something a little more substantial. Like passed hors d'oeuvres. People are so stingy, though."

"You might get your wish," Iris said. "The museum *was* an old fish processing plant. Maybe we'll get crab cakes!"

They didn't bother with driving. The new museum was only a twenty-minute walk away. It was a lovely spring evening, and the sky had taken on a silver-blue sheen. That's when Iris saw the first ghost of the night. At least, she thought it was a ghost. The shape it had wasn't particularly human. It was a translucent blob of color smeared on the surface of the world. She could see right through its cobweb-thin substance. It had no features. No eyes, no face, no hands, no legs. But Iris knew that it was once a human being, and that it was watching the two of them amble down the street.

"What is it?" Tamar said. That's when Iris noticed that she had stopped walking. She was tempted to tell her "nothing," but Tamar could always see right through her.

"I'm just seeing one of the caspers," she replied. The splotch of color, coral pink, made no move toward the two of them. It just hung in the air.

"Does this one have a collapsed face? A missing eye?" Iris shook her head. "Then I ain't interested," Tamar said. "I like my haints to be walking hot messes."

They both laughed. "Girl, you're a trip," Iris said.

"I try," Tamar said. They moved past the vague wisp, on down the street. "I still think you should try to communicate with the caspers. By the way, what did this one look like?"

She told Tamar that it was just a hazy shape. "They're no better than hallucinations," Iris said. "I can't talk to them, and they can't talk to me."

"What about that girl? What was her name—Ruby?"

"Pearl."

"That's right. You were able to talk to her."

"Ha! Only if you call random images flashing in your brain 'talking!'"

Tamar said, "People pay good money to hear mediums. And those mediums just piece together some mumbo jumbo, and folks just eat it up. Dionne Warwick rakes it in."

"I'm not Dionne Warwick," Iris said. "So nobody is lining up to hear Madame Iris. Besides, it's uncomfortable. I couldn't tell which thoughts were mine, and which were hers. It's not a nice feeling."

They walked in silence for a minute or two. The museum was finally in view in the distance, a low building that spilled out bright light onto the lapping waters of the nearby pier. It had been under construction since they moved to Shimmer, and it seemed like it would never open. It had barely been on Iris's radar. Adjusting to small-town life, finding a job and dealing with Ernie's orneriness had drained her. Tamar was more interested; back in Baltimore she'd always arrange trips to the museums in the city and nearby DC.

"You know, people lived in the marsh," said Tamar.

"Huh? What does that have to do with anything?"

"I think that's why you keep seeing these caspers. People lived in the marsh, to escape being slaves. I read about it in that article about Hazel Whitby. One of the reasons this one dude thinks she made those tapestries was that she was dreaming of escape. And the marsh was a place where she could disappear."

"Seems like a stretch."

"Maybe," Tamar said. "But there were some folks who lived in the marsh, and I imagine they died there, too. Maybe that's why you see them by the water."

"Way to bring down the mood, T."

Tamar said nothing. Was she sulking? Iris didn't think so. Tamar's gait was free and easy, her face calm. It didn't matter anyway. The new museum was close.

They saw that there was a line to get inside. This was not surprising. Every Shimmer resident had gotten an invitation in the mail. Tamar and Iris joined the line, right behind Samuel and Eileen Miller, their across-the-street neighbors.

"They're letting groups in only when a certain number of people leave," said Eileen.

Samuel said, "I hope that the artwork is worth it."

Tamar said, "Well, it's a nice enough night."

The line moved at a snail's pace. Both couples exchanged their summer plans, neighborhood business and family news. They learned that Eileen's father was exhibiting some symptoms of Alzheimer's, and Tamar gave them advice.

"Don't argue with him if he starts accusing you of things," Tamar said. "Just go along with it."

Iris was only half listening, though. She saw two more abstract spirit things around the museum. An arm hovered above the reeds in the lapping water. The silhouette of a head drifted up and down the line, as if searching for someone. They were both the same awful shade of magenta, the color of azaleas. She checked her watch. It was nearly twenty minutes. They had barely moved.

Samuel said what she'd been thinking. "All right now. I don't want to be here all night."

Tamar said, "It will be worth it. I've been following the museum since I moved to Shimmer." Her voice rose up in pitch. She had the same excited look she'd had when she discovered fado music, or the fiction of Octavia Butler. "Both Hazel and Shadrach are spiritual precursors to the Color Field movement. You know, artists like Morris Louis, or Sam Gilliam. Remember the Gilliam exhibit we saw at the Corcoran, Iris?"

"Yes." Tamar had dragged her down to DC a year or two ago to see a retrospective of Gilliam's work. Iris remembered the brightly hued splotches of color on canvas and folded bits of fabric. His work was joyous, the colors luminous. She had told Tamar that it looked like he was trying to paint music.

"Well, Hazel's quilts—they're really tapestries—and Grayson's paintings all capture the Shimmer Marsh, but in an abstract way. And these two artists had no training whatsoever!"

Samuel Miller looked unimpressed. Iris felt a tinge of embarrassment for her girlfriend. But mostly, she felt a surge of warmth. Tamar was so cute when she geeked out.

Eileen had looked away from them. "Look," she said. "Finally. The line is moving!"

Inside the Whitby-Grayson Museum were a couple of circular tables in the center that were laden with various appetizers. There was the requisite cheese and cracker plate, a fruit tray (grapes, strawberries and chunks of cantaloupe), a bread bowl filled with a green dip and ringed with slices of baguette and a tray of vegetables nested in a bed of curly kale. Music drifted out of hidden speakers, the languorous voice of Sade. A cash bar was set up to one side. The museum was airy and spacious, which was not surprising. The owners planned to double the museum as an event space.

"Genie Francis is over by the information desk," Tamar whispered in her ear. Iris observed a tall white woman in a tailored black pantsuit. The woman had silver spiky hair and dangling dagger earrings, both of which suited her severe, angular features. Though her outfit was relatively plain, the lady oozed of wealth and privilege.

"I'm gonna wander about," Tamar told her, then made her way through the crowd to the walls. Iris followed suit after she ate a couple of canapés.

Iris didn't know what to expect. Art was Tamar's bailiwick. Tamar's apartment had been filled with coffee table books. She had so many that she had several towers of them stacked on the floor. Iris made her get rid of some of them when they moved to Shimmer.

She started to view the work before her. She saw a piece of fabric, primitively embroidered, with strips of blue, green and spattered with drops of a vivid pink color. Iris did not like it, for some reason. The color was too bright to be an artifact from the late 1800s, and there was something off about the stitch work, something she couldn't put a name to. Iris leaned forward, thinking a closer examination was in order. The wave of discomfort she felt for these quilts or tapestries was overwhelming.

It happened in a blink. Between the flickering strobe of the overhead lightbulb, and a pulse of her heartbeat, she was no longer in the Whitby-Grayson Museum, in a room with people carrying plastic cups of wine and paper plates full of miniature crab cakes. The ambient din of conversation, the press of perfumed bodies all fell away and were replaced. Iris was transported to somewhere else, somewhere far away from Shimmer.

Iris stood in a marsh that seemed to go on forever. But the perspective was skewed. The sun, for instance, was too big, and too orange. The grassy hillocks where the deep green of forest moss, and the turquoise water was crystal clear. Schools of fish with enameled scales darted in the clear waters, along with silently patrolling giant catfish. The sky above was deep azure. The grass was dotted here and there with strange flowers, ones that were a pink so intense, it almost hurt the eye.

"Excuse me," Iris heard someone say, and was back in the museum, in front of one of the tapestries. Dazed, she moved aside to let a white lady in stiletto heels glance at the artwork.

She moved down, past a couple of hangings that had clusters of folks around them until she found a quilt that was relatively free of gawkers.

She stared the floor, at the wall space around the hanging. At the acrylic box that housed Whitby's work. *I really shouldn't look,* she thought. *I should just leave this museum, leave the weirdness behind. I should tell Tamar about what just happened, where I went.*

Iris found herself looking at the new quilt, in spite of her reservations. She wasn't sure why. Maybe this—what?—astral projection thing was interesting.

She found herself back in the marsh again, with its dreamlike colors. This time, she wasn't alone. She saw a man in the distance, on a small hillock away from her. He stood before a canvas, but he wasn't painting. Rather, a landscape slowly formed, daubs of paint building in layers. On another patch of dry land, there was a woman who sat at a table. She was making tiny dresses. Iris watched as the woman added sequins to a taffeta gown. Another man was fishing in the turquoise waters. He reeled in a large net from the water. Fish weren't in the net. Instead, there were glistening glass bottles. All of the people wore outfits in that same sickeningly pink color. The marsh was like a distorted Shimmer Marsh, one that was put through funhouse mirrors and oversaturated. At the same time, it felt real. She could smell the brackish water, and heard the cries of seabirds as they wheeled above in the cloudless sky.

"Pardon me!" Iris snapped out of the hallucination, found her sense of balance was off kilter. She stumbled, was caught by the wrist by a tall brown-skinned man with a hi-top fade.

"I'm so sorry," she said, embarrassed.

"Don't worry about it, child. This art has the same effect on me!"

"How do you mean?" Iris observed him with interest. What if he were like she was—what if he could *see* things?

"Those colors, they make me seasick. I'm photosensitive, you know." The man laughed. "TMI, I know."

Iris smiled, and thanked him for catching her.

She avoided the walls for a moment, to gain her composure. She escaped to the middle of the room, grabbed some ice water and gulped it down. She was sweating and cold at the same time. And also, she was exhilarated. The tapestries made her feel helium-headed, and sugar-rushed. It was a jolt of caffeine that was just below the point of being jittery. When Pearl invaded her body and soul, it had felt the same way. Weird, but not unpleasant. A tingle that started at the scalp and then marched down her spine, like ants with feet of needles. It was delicious, warm, and cooling all at once.

She had to tell Tamar about this. Iris wove through the crowd, careful not to look directly at the art on the wall. She couldn't find her anywhere. Anxiety struck, like a lick of lightning through her brain. It was doused when she saw Tamar in the other room—the Shadrach Grayson gallery.

The artwork in this room looked different. Oil paint slathered thickly on wooden boards in layers of green and black and silver, twilight colors. A giant purple-pink sphere dominated the center of this paintings, hovering above the abstract landscapes like an alien sun. But it had the same quivering energy as Hazel's work. Iris felt a flutter throughout her body.

She sidled up to Tamar, who was looking at one of the larger paintings.

Tamar said, without glancing away from the painting, "They don't know where Hazel got the fabric color for her quilts. Or where Shadrach got his paints. It's not like people just gave slaves art supplies."

"Not like they just had the money, either," Iris said.

She let Tamar absorb the picture in silence. She thought, *I'll tell her about the strangeness of the paintings on the way home.* Iris didn't want to spoil her joy. She looked away from the painting on the wall. The light in this gallery was dark and subdued. It seemed to bring out the undertones in everything. Her black dress looked blue, and Tamar's peach dress and the pink hibiscus in her hair looked magenta.

Tamar said, "I also love the way the fuchsia globes move. It's almost as if they are trying to escape."

Iris looked at the picture in front of her, an involuntary response to Tamar's words.

She was thrown into the world of the painting. Black earth, silver-green reeds, dark blue water in between. And above, the moon, vivid and purple. It was much bigger than a moon. It was closer to the earth, just out of reach. Without thinking, Iris walked toward the moon. She walked on wet earth and through water, but she didn't get wet, or stained. The fuchsia moon got closer and closer, bigger and bigger. And the closer she got, the less it looked like a moon. The texture was all wrong. The striations were not crater-like. There were flute-shaped mouths, each flute disgorging a pair of dark red antennae-like stamens. It was a flower—a cluster of them. The moon was a giant marsh-bell!

Then, it moved. Unfolded. Flowerets melding together. Protruding stamens disappearing. The tiny flutes became one giant flute, the shape and texture of a piece of fabric. She saw a brown face in the middle of shifting floral orb—

"…Iris!"

She heard Tamar's voice from far away. She wasn't the voice of the woman in the moon flower thing. Iris knew that her voice was different. Tamar's voice drowned out the sound of the frogs and crickets. The sound of the marsh.

"Iris!"

The marsh faded. Slowly. Layer by layer of paint. She almost saw the face. The Face of the Flower, the face of the color. Iris reached up.

And found herself reaching for—

Nothing. Tamar stood next to her, her face crumbled with concern. It took Iris a moment or two to get her bearings. She was here, in the museum, in Shimmer. A group of concerned people ringed around them.

"Is she all right?" Iris heard distantly.

"Iris, honey, speak to me."

She found her voice. It was buried, beneath the soil of the painting, in that marsh that was and was not the Shimmer Marsh.

"I'm…fine," she said. "I just need some air."

Iris moved through the crowd, and Tamar followed her. Once she reached the outside of the museum, Iris took a deep breath. It cleared her head, and she started sorting the images that had flowed from the artwork. The work was full of spirits, and Iris wasn't sure that they were human ones. The woman/flower/moon apparition felt alien. There had been no recognizable emotion there, no taint of sadness or joy or wonder. Just a naked and endless demand. An imperative, one that resounded throughout her brain.

"You okay?" Tamar asked. "What happened back in there?"

"I don't know," Iris said. She paused a moment, trying to find the right words to describe the cloying, clawing presence she had felt. That thrilling, roiling color that spoke and moved through the artwork. She finally turned to face Tamar, after gazing out on the marsh from the museum's pier.

Tamar was enrobed in a transparent film of fuchsia. It swirled around her, gossamer-thin. Everything was filtered through this translucent veil, and stained by it. The whites of Tamar's eyes, and her teeth, all faintly purple-pink.

"Are you all right?" Tamar repeated. Concern was etched on her face. She silently watched the veil ripple like the marsh waters.

"I'm going home, I think," Iris said.

"Do you mind if I stay a little longer?"

"Not at all. I'll be fine."

***

When Iris got home, she headed straight for the kitchen. She found only a half-full carton of iodized table salt in the cupboard. There was no indication whether it was from the land or the sea. It certainly wasn't blessed, like the salt from the botánica had been those years ago. But it was all she had. She sprinkled the entirety of the salt on the threshold of the door, even though she knew it probably wouldn't work.

She was restless, so she made a cup of chamomile tea, and added a touch of rum for good measure. She sat in the living room, tried to slow her breathing and savor the herb tea. Iris wasn't scared, not exactly. She was weirdly excited. Her head swam with images of the ghost marsh. It had been so beautiful, the colors there were vibrant. A wild euphoria rose in her chest, like a bubble. The bubble lay just beneath her heart, which began to pound.

I want to go there again, she thought. She also knew that the magic world conjured by the spirit was dangerously tantalizing. It was a sugar rush, over-saturated, and so beautiful that it would make the real world seem washed out, a pale copy of the lustrous richness. The real Shimmer Marsh was full of sulfurous smells, mud, and biting insects. Many times she'd seen the rotting carcasses of sea birds or dead crabs in the muck. People threw garbage into its waters, and things died there, an endless churning cycle of life and death, rebirth and waste. That marsh was a fairyland where everything was perfect, maybe even better than perfect. It was an idealized landscape. Nothing ever died there, or rotted. It was a pristine paradise.

So why am I terrified?

It was the intensity and hunger of the woman who hid in those works of art that scared her. The welter of visions had been strong, tsunami-strong. They had overpowered Iris, to the point that there was no Iris. She wasn't even sure that the woman she saw hidden in the flower, in the color, actually *was* a woman. She was a force of nature, like the wind or the rain or the sky itself. The concept of ghost, spirit, or phantom was not adequate. She was energy, given a vaguely human form. Was she an angel? Or—was she something else?

The lock in the door sounded, snapping Iris out of her frantic reverie. She almost dropped her tea. Which was stupid and dramatic.

Keep it together, Iris Marie.

Tamar stood in the door frame. She was draped in curtains of fuchsia gossamer. It was so beautiful, the way it shimmered, and enfolded her girlfriend. Tamar was a goddess, caught up in a brilliant halo. She was on fire. Then she stepped over the threshold.

Tamar stumbled. The gossamer veil burned away, became mist.

"Tamar!" Iris was up and by her side in a moment. "Are you okay?"

Tamar steadied herself. "I think so. I don't know what happened.

I think I had a hot flash. I'm too young to be going through The Change!"

"Sit down," said Iris, guiding her to the sofa. "I'll get you a glass of water."

After Tamar had taken a couple of fortifying sips, Iris took her hand, and told her about what she had experienced in the museum.

"So, you think it's Pearl, the sequel?" Tamar asked.

Iris laughed. "Girl, you crazy. But I think this casper is different. Pearl was a collection of images, memories, impressions. You could see the human in her. I don't think that Pearl wanted to take me over as much as borrow me. This one, this fuchsia-toned casper, doesn't think like a person. There are no memories. No emotions. There is just the marsh. The same vision, forever."

"What did she want with me? Why did she wrap me in that aura?"

"I think she wants you to recreate the marsh. To bring it to life, to make it real. You said that there was a group of artists who were all inspired by the marsh, and the marsh-bell, right?"

Tamar nodded.

"Well, I think she *is* the marsh. Or at least, she thinks she is."

"Well, she would be sorely disappointed. I can hardly draw stick figures!" Tamar emitted a bark of laughter. "So, the ghost of Hazel Whitby wants to take up residence in me."

"I don't think it's Hazel, though. Or, if it is, she's been warped to the point where her memories are gone. I can usually get some sense of who the caspers once were. But this one is just a color, that particular color."

"A Colored spirit," said Tamar.

"Girl, stop. This is serious." Tamar stopped smiling, putting a stoic look on her face. "I don't think you should visit the museum. Not until I can figure out what's happening."

***

The first tarot card she drew was the High Priestess. She was at work, in the hotel gift shop, and as was the case in midweek, the store was empty. Everything was stocked, and the displays were pristine. There was nothing to do. Iris bought herself a book of word jumbles, but got bored a quarter of the way through. Her boss, Isabel Campbell, would have a fit if she caught Iris reading. Isabel wanted to see people busy, and a word jumble at least looked like Iris was writing, from a distance. Isabel would emerge from her office lair every other hour or so to patrol the hotel lobby. You could hear her coming by the clickety-clacking of her stilettos.

Iris put aside the book of jumbles. She still held her pen. For some reason, she could not put it down. It felt right in her hand, poised to make a mark of some kind. There was a legal pad nearby that she used for jotting notes down. She pulled it toward her, putting the point of the pen to the paper.

The girl runs back to the marsh with the things that she has stolen from the Taylors. In her sack, there are apples, cheese, a heel of bread, a bottle of wine, flint, matches, and candles. The moon is hiding behind a wall of clouds, so she has to make her way back to the marsh by touch and muscle memory. That one was a close call. Her rummaging had woken up one hound, and soon, the others were baying in excitement. She heard Eliza Taylor call out just as she finished swiping the food in the larders. The Taylors must have just gotten some dogs; she doesn't recall them before. The Smythes and the McCallisters had mean dogs, ones that could smell you a mile away, so their homes were off limits. Which was a shame. Alden Smythe had the best collection of pens and paper in the whole county. Once, she had stolen an entirely blank journal. The smell of the paper, its thick texture, the smell of the leather binding and the glue had nearly sent her over into delirium. Was there anything more precious than paper, waiting to be filled with ink? The Taylors only had black ink and only loose sheets of the cheapest paper available. They rattled in her bag, along with her other treasures.

It wasn't until she heard the clicking of Isabel's heels that Iris looked up. She slipped the legal pad in the cubby hole beneath the cash register. The mundane world returned, the cash register and the banks of overpriced candy came into focus.

Isabel came into the store, and gave Iris a new task—to help with the reconciliation.

***

A week or so later, on a Saturday, Iris found herself alone in the house. Tamar had gone out to the farmer's market a couple of towns away. The Amish set up a stand in the Chesapeake town, and their baked goods sold out fast. Tamar went early every other Saturday to stock up. Iris knew that Tamar would probably go clothes shopping; there were a couple of thrift shops on the way.

She pulled out the slip of legal paper she had folded and placed into her purse. She spread it out on the coffee table in front of her, smoothing it of crinkles. Her mindless doodle was a version of a tarot card. Tamar given her a couple of books on the subject. The high priestess in this doodle had a round face, the face of the girl from her vision, a wild afro, and flowing purple-pink robes. Iris didn't have a purple or pink pen at work, or at home. She touched the paper. She felt a vibration, faint, when she touched the drawing. It was pleasant, like a soft breeze or the feel of silk. The urge to hold a pen, to make a mark on paper, returned. Ernest Dupré would have disapproved. Well, fuck Ernest Dupré, and her mother for that matter.

Iris went searching in the kitchen drawers. She unearthed a small spiral notebook that was mostly blank. The first few pages were filled with To Do lists. She pulled out a pen, and closed her eyes.

The girl sits at the feet of the old woman, ostensibly to help her. But the old woman seems to be doing fine. The old woman is enormous, like a giant in a fairytale. She is ancient, and might have been 300 pounds or more. The dress she wears is as big as a tent. The girl can imagine getting lost in the swirl of her petticoats. Her skin is red and mottled, and her face has weird growths on it, like mushroom caps. A few steely grey hairs escape from her bonnet. Ma'am Fiona was a fearsome sight when the girl first saw her. The other children called her the Ogress, but since the girl has known her, she is no longer afraid of her. Fiona the Ogress is quite kind. Fiona calls her "brownie," every now and then, and it took the girl a while to realize that she wasn't referring to the girl's skin color. She dozes half the time the girl is supposed to watch over her, and lets out bullfrog-deep snores. Other times, she gives the girl boiled sweets or pieces of cake. And sometimes, she tells her stories from the Old Country.

As far as the girl can tell, the Old Country was a land of perpetual mists, rains, and bogs. It was full of strange beasts, like seals who could become women, or men would can change into horses. The Old Country was a place haunted by ghosts, the spirits of people who were marked for death and sacrificed to the peat bogs.

"The bog kept their bodies fresh," Fiona told her once. "But their spirits were restless. Heathenish practices were common in the old days."

The Ogress wakes up from a brief nap with a swinish snort. The girl had been playing with a rag doll—another one of Fiona's unexpected gifts. She drops the doll and makes sure that the Ogress is comfortable. They are sitting on the front port of the MacCubbins' house, which faces the marsh. Twilight stains the sky.

"We best be getting inside before the mosquitoes start coming around," says Madame Fiona in her lilting accented voice. The girl

knows that getting her inside will be a chore in itself, mostly getting her out of the chair.

The girl points to something. A glowing light is dancing over the reeds. It's like a tiny star, a bright ball of light that cuts a swathe through the wetlands.

Fiona squints. "That's a will-o'-the-wisp. They're beautiful, but they are also deadly. They lead people into the deeper marshlands, and leave them there to die."

The girl has a hard time believing this is true. The light was so beautiful. There was nothing sinister about it, or the marsh, as far as the girl is concerned. It was like a giant firefly, all golden-green.

"Iris!"

Tamar's yell pulled her from the vision. Tamar was leaning down into her face, and vigorously shaking her shoulder. At first she was confused, as the mundane world of the kitchen came back into focus. Then, for one second, Iris felt a flare of anger. Tamar had severed her connection with the nameless girl. How dare she!

"…there, I thought you were having a fit," Tamar was saying. She was so loud. Even the bracelets she wore were irritating. "What were you doing?"

Iris found herself unable to speak. Words wouldn't come. There was no real way to explain the glorious link she felt, or the vividness of the image. She knew Fiona, her thick brogue, her homely warmth, her thrilling stories of the Old Country. She could smell the marsh air, the salt, the sweet, the sulfurous.

Tamar didn't wait for Iris to speak, though. She grabbed the piece of paper she had written on. "What the hell is this?" Tamar said.

Iris looked down at the paper. It was covered in ink, in some places quite thickly. At first she couldn't make sense of it. It was a mix of fluid lines and squiggly ornaments, endlessly mirroring themselves. Here and there, through the spiky jungle of black ink, were bright spots of fuchsia. The color seemed to burn through the paper.

Iris said, "I'm so sorry, my love. She is here."

Tamar looked confused. Then she said, "You mean the Colored Spirit?"

Iris said, "Look."

Her finger pointed towards a face, hidden in the riot of black and fuchsia. It was in the web of Iris's work. For now.

19: ENSEMBLE

XAVIER

"He just used Magic Markers," said Gladys Winston as she handed Xavier a cup of coffee. "Nothing fancy." Mrs. Winston (née Quarles) was in her late sixties. Her silver hair was pulled back by a scrunchie. It contrasted nicely with her dark skin. Her face was unlined, but her neck was wrinkled. She wore a blue floral muumuu and flip-flops. Xavier could smell the flowery, old lady perfume she wore; it was the same as his own grandmother's. Mrs. Winston had been excited over the phone to show him her father's work. "It's at least as good as that stuff in the museum," she'd told him. "But they don't want it because of his one mistake."

Xavier couldn't disagree. Hosea Quarles's work was spread out on the living room coffee table. All of the work was contained in several oversized scrapbooks, with each page encased in plastic. Hosea's chosen canvas was graph paper. Xavier sat on the plastic-covered sofa, sorting through the images. Lenski had not done the work justice. The shapes of the letters were somewhere between cuneiform and hieroglyphics. The wedge-like shapes almost became recognizable forms, like the head of a blossom, or the crescent moon. Like all of the Shimmer artists' work, it was both

177

carefully crafted and woefully amateurish. Was that supposed to be a feather? And that weird, ridged shell-thing kind of looked like a small A. Also, Xavier knew that this scrawl of bright marker wasn't just a meaningless jumble of pseudo letters. What did they mean? Were the letters invocations, or praise songs? Or were they a curse, a malediction, or a warning? There was a tropical sensibility to the shapes, one that summoned a vegetable heaven, a fungal realm that grew in his mind. He felt ants move beneath his skin, and then, a rain of cold needles like bad acupuncture piercing him.

"Do you mind if I take some pictures of these?"

Mrs. Winston consented. As Xavier snapped pictures, she said, "You know, he wasn't in his right mind when he did it. None 'em were. In my humble opinion."

"How do you mean?"

"It was a cult. At least, that's what my mother said."

1958

It started with James Olds, the bottle tree artist, Gladys (Quarles) Winston told Xavier. He was a loner who lived in a trailer out by the marsh, where his house faced the old Whitby manse. He was a strange man, who lived what would now be called an 'off the grid' lifestyle. Mr. Olds was a peculiar-looking man. He was tall and bony, and he walked with a pronounced limp. He'd served in the Korean War, and the feeling was that when he came back, he wasn't right in the head. Rumor had it that he had been dishonorably discharged on a morals charge. You would see Mr. Olds limping around town and back to his marsh-side shack all the time. People called him the Scarecrow of Shimmer. Even to his face! And he didn't seem to mind at all. When she was young, Gladys just just knew him as Old Scarecrow. He was friendly enough, though he would mutter to himself on his many trips back and forth to his ramshackle home.

Mr. Olds began collecting glass bottles one spring. All types: soda bottles, medicine bottles, wine and liquor. He would roam around town with a battered shopping cart, picking up bottles from trash cans and behind stores. Sometimes, you would see him along the highway shoulder, picking them up, muttering to himself. Some people saved bottles for him, and gave them to him when he trundled around. Gladys's father, Hosea, was one of those people. Hosea Quarles was a heavy drinker. Her folks went through bottles of gin and whiskey quickly. Her mother, Doreen, would always have a drink ready for him when Hosea came home, a g&t or a dirty martini. Both of them smoked, as well. Gladys didn't have friends over because she was embarrassed by her perennially tipsy parents. ("I don't drink or smoke, to this day," she told Xavier.) Luckily, her parents were the jovial kind of drunks.

One evening, Scarecrow dropped by and Hosea gave him an empty Johnnie Walker bottle, the kind that looks like a genie's bottle. The two of them got to talking—about the current war (Vietnam) and the one they'd both served in. (Hosea had been stationed in Germany the same time.) When he wasn't mumbling to himself, Mr. Olds was quite charming and intelligent. He had strong opinions—about civil rights and the current direction of the country. Hosea eventually asked him, over cigars and bourbon, what exactly Olds used the bottles for. Olds responded by inviting Hosea to see for himself. "I don't get very many visitors," Scarecrow said.

Later that week, Hosea did just that. Scarecrow's house was a silver Airstream that he kept shiny so that when the sunlight hit it just right, it blinded you. It was small inside, with barely enough room for two people. Scarecrow had to stoop down because he was so tall, and Hosea was a big man, built like a football player. The inside of the house was as spotless as the outside. That's when Hosea saw the bottles Mr. Olds collected. They were transformed.

Some were painted, both in solid colors and patterns. Some of the painted bottles had shards of glass, beads and sequins affixed to them, and others were wrapped what looked like wallpaper or gift wrap. One bottle was affixed with shells, and another had the delicate mouthlike flowerets of a marsh-bell encrusted on its side with wax drippings. All of them were in the same palette range, a purple-red color. The color of sissies. Hosea thought these crafts were beautiful, in an odd way. He said so—the first part, about being beautiful, not the part about being odd.

"What inspired you?" he asked Old Scarecrow.

"I'll show you," he replied. "And you will see it, or you will not."

"See what?" Hosea Quarles was a no-nonsense kind of man. To him, the most beautiful thing in the world was a car in perfect condition, the engine purring like a cat, the paint job showroom shiny and flawless, the chassis architecturally sound. He wasn't into artsy-fartsy stuff, or mystical mumbo jumbo, and this statement was too close to that for comfort. In the end, though, Hosea was a polite man and let Old Scarecrow lead him to the ruins of the old house on the edge of the marsh.

It was still standing, but it was in poor repair. The front veranda was more or less intact, though it was covered by creepers. More of Old Scarecrow's bottles were lined up against the house. Maybe fifty, or hundred or even more. All of them had a section that was painted or woven or stamped on with that magenta color. The color of lilacs, azaleas, bougainvillea, and the marsh-bell orchid. The color was so intense that it glowed through the darkening twilight.

"James, why are we here?" Hosea asked.

"Watch," Old Scarecrow replied, pointing toward the marsh. "And stay quiet. She don't show herself to everybody."

Hosea was on the verge of saying something, but what would be the use? The Negro was crazy. The rumored morals charge floated up in his brain, so he made sure that Old Scarecrow was always in front of him. Old Scarecrow just gazed out at the marsh as the sun set. It might have been an hour. Every time Hosea got antsy, Mr. Olds said something like, "It won't be long, now." Thankfully, the nights were getting much longer so they didn't wait for too long before the sky darkened.

After a few minutes, Hosea said, "I've waited long enough. I have to get home to my family. I promised Gladys that I would read a bedtime story to her, and…"

His voice trailed off, because he saw it.

What was it, though? It was a floating light that moved through the marsh grasses, heading toward the house. It moved delicately like a dandelion's seed head, but it was as bright as a firework explosion. He couldn't keep his eyes off it, as it cut through the marsh. The ball of magenta light never reached the veranda. It hovered a discreet distance away. It stayed there a good while, as a thousand unasked questions piled up in his head. He thought it was beautiful, a lacy filigree thing. He thought of Tinker Bell, the tiny fairy from *Peter Pan*. Then, he thought that he was going insane, like Old Scarecrow next to him. Maybe it was contagious.

After a while it—she—left, and skittered across the expanse of the Shimmer Marsh. She moved through the air as if it were water, and she was one of those bioluminescent deep-sea jellyfish.

"I have to leave," Hosea said as soon as it (she) winked out. Old Scarecrow said nothing as he walked Hosea back to his car. He didn't think about what he saw as he drove home. What was there to think about? What he had seen must have been some trick. Maybe Old Scarecrow's mobile home had some sort of weird gas leak that caused hallucinations. Or the orb was just some kind of mutant lightning bug. Back home, Doreen asked him what had happened at James Olds's house.

"Negro is nuttier than a fruitcake," Hosea told his wife. "He turned all of those bottles into some kind of arts and crafts kinda thing. He believes that some ghost woman told him to make them."

He neglected to tell her that he might have seen the ghost woman.

Doreen said, "I don't want that man in our house anymore. He's harmless enough, but he could go psycho at any moment. I've read all about schizophrenics." (Doreen read True Crime magazines avidly. There was a stack of them in the john.)

Hosea agreed with her, and put the matter out of his mind. When Old Scarecrow came around, he left the wine and liquor bottles in the garbage. The old fool could get them from there if he wanted them so much.

Most of the year passed by without Hosea Quarles thinking about the weird incident. He had a couple of dreams about the will-o'-the-wisp thing, nothing too major. Nothing Doreen or Gladys knew about. He developed a distinct dislike of the color magenta, though. He outright told Doreen that one of her new evening gowns, which was that shade, was ugly. Doreen returned the gown the next day. Gladys went through a pink phase, like most girls her age. Every now and then one of her toys or barrettes strayed into that color range, and he felt the mildest discomfort.

Gladys expressed interest in piano lessons that year. Every Saturday morning, Doreen drove their nine-year-old daughter to Edna Wray's house, which faced the Shimmer Marsh but was still in town. Doreen went up to New York for a Broadway show one weekend, and instead of sleeping in, Hosea had to take his daughter to her lesson. The lesson only lasted one hour. Mrs. Wray welcomed him to stay for the duration in her kitchen, where she had coffee and some danish he was welcome to have.

There was a curio cabinet full of dolls in the living room on the way to the kitchen. It was something that he wouldn't have noticed, save for one thing. All of the dolls wore outfits all in that ghastly pink-purple color. Hoop skirts, pencil skirts, ruffled blouses, evening gowns, all of them, lurid magenta. All of the doll women were Negroes. He could see that some of them had been white, blond-haired porcelain dolls, but someone—Edna?—had glazed their skin brown.

She don't show herself to everybody.

Hosea found himself standing in the Shimmer Marsh. He knew that it wasn't the real Shimmer Marsh, because the colors were too intensely saturated, as if someone had painted upon the grasses and waters, making them luminous. Also, there was no humidity in the air or wetness by his feet. The water was clear as crystal, the muddy depths smooth as a swimming pool bottom. Fish swam in the water, minnows the color of gold or silver coins, trout with iridescent scales, and catfish the size of a child. Birds glided through the mauve sky, eagles and terns and herons. The grassy islets were inundated with marsh-bells, their circular multi-trumpeted heads rising above the marsh grass like miniature suns.

Also, he wasn't alone.

The doll woman, Scarecrow's pink orb, they were the same. The woman was young, not more than twenty, and her hair was a wooly dark bush. The shape of her hair reminded him of the clumps of leaves in baobab trees in Africa. Her hair had the same witchy, organic quality.

"Who are you," he said, even though he knew she wasn't real.

She told him.

The words blew past in strange shapes. It went by his ears in a storm of petals, color and sound that he could only just grasp.

"...Daddy?"

Gladys's voice bought him back to Edna Wray's living room. He was so disoriented, he wobbled on his feet.

"Have a seat, Mr. Quarles. Gladys, go and get your father a glass of juice. I have orange juice and lemonade in the fridge. Go on, now."

As soon as Gladys went into the kitchen, Mrs. Wray said, in a low tone, "You saw *her*, didn't you?"

He didn't bother to deny this. Instead, he asked, "Who is she?"

"She's an angel, of course!"

Just at that moment Gladys returned with the glass of juice, which Hosea gulped down in a hurry and left Edna's house. Back at home, he thought, *The swamp drives people crazy.* Then he thought, *What if Edna is right? What if she is angel? But angels don't travel in pink bubbles, like the Good Witch in The Wizard of Oz.* Mostly, though, he wanted the whole business out of his mind.

But as hard as he tried, his mind kept drifting back to that tranquil technicolor marsh, to that orb, to those dolls and those transformed liquor bottles.

***

"Daddy began drawing the things not long after," Gladys told Xavier. She was a wonderful storyteller, and chose the right words with the precision of a jeweler. Xavier could practically see the story unfold in front of him, like a movie. "He only drew on Sundays, because, you see, he thought that she was angel, just like Edna Wray said."

"Did Scarecrow—Mr. Olds—think she was an angel?" Xavier asked. He sipped the tea Gladys Winston provided. The teacups and saucers were all milky green Jadeite, something that Dr. Giordano would geek out about. He was into Populuxe aesthetics.

"I don't think that he did think she was especially divine," Gladys Winston said. Her eyes weren't on him. "He thought that she was a nature spirit of some kind, connected somehow to the marsh-bell orchid.

"Anyway, the three of them became as thick as thieves. They would hang out at the old Whitby place, waiting for her to visit them. I guess she was a kind of a muse to them. A spirit that inspired them to make artwork."

"What did other people think of their work?"

"Bear in mind, Xavier, that Daddy wanted to keep this secret, and, to a certain extent, so did Mrs. Wray. She believed that they—Daddy, Old Scarecrow and herself—were chosen, like Biblical prophets. Like Job and Jonah and Ezekiel. Old Scarecrow thought of his art as a gift, custom made for her. Not to be shared. And Daddy, well, he thought he was writing down the words she'd say to him, during his visions. Words in a forgotten language."

Xavier thought about the Mystery cults built around Greek and Egyptian deities in ancient times, or the secret ceremonies of orixa worshippers. He'd seen YouTube videos of people speaking in tongues, their bodies controlled by invisible entities.

"Did he ever talk about them—the visions?"

"Not to me. But there was this one time… Bear in mind, I was little, maybe eleven or so, and I overheard Mama and Daddy fight. She'd accused him of going off the deep end, like James Olds. And Mrs. Wray had always been a little off since her husband ran off with a white woman. She would insist that she was a widow, even though people saw him down in DC with his white girlfriend. He told Mama that he *had* to keep drawing. 'She's telling me her story,' he said. I never forgot that."

Xavier flipped through the scrapbook. What story did the words tell?

"That's when Mama called the group a cult," Gladys continued. "She said that the marsh woman had driven Edna Wray and Old Scarecrow crazy. Now, it was driving him insane. Daddy was stubborn, though. He accused Mama of being a shrew, and kept on visiting the Whitby mansion. Mama canceled my piano lessons; she thought Mrs. Wray was a bad influence."

"So, it was a kind of…artists' salon they had there, out in Shimmer Marsh?" Xavier could see them all working on the porch of the decayed mansion, waiting for the woman's spirit to manifest.

"I guess," Gladys replied. "I just know Daddy and them other two hung out so much that kids at school used to tease me. They said that Daddy had a screw loose. I even got into a fight with a boy once. Got sent home, and everything!"

"Why did your dad—Mr. Quarles—burn down the Whitby manse?"

"He told me why years later, when Mama had passed."

***

Every time he worked on his art, Hosea Quarles would see the marsh and the sole inhabitant of it. He could more than just see it. He felt the breeze on his skin, smelled the salt air. Each sensation became another shape in the magenta woman's strange alphabet, a shape he was compelled to commit to paper. Edna Wray described her moments with the magenta woman as sacred. The dolls she made were avatars in her honor, a way to thank her for blessing Edna with her presence. And James Olds talked about the magenta woman as if she were his girlfriend.

At first, the two men thought she was the ghost of Hazel Whitby. (Wray stuck to the angel theory.) Olds didn't think so. "I think she's much older than Hazel," he told them one night. "Sometimes, she shows me scenes from her life. Or at least, I think they are. The point is, she might have inspired Hazel Whitby, like she inspired us."

When Hosea saw her world, he'd called out the name "Hazel." The image of the marsh-bell flashed in his mind. *Marsh-bell? Marcia Bell? Magenta? Fuchsia?* Was that her name? When she appeared to them, like a stemless marsh-bell when the three met in Shimmer Marsh, who or what she was hardly mattered. Whether she was an angel or a ghost, she radiated euphoria, and they, in turn, tried to capture it and mirror it back through their works.

Hosea initially worked on his art on Sundays. But that began to change. He would work for an hour or two. Soon, it became the whole afternoon. One time, Gladys saw her father working in his study.

("I saw him working with his eyes closed," she said to Xavier, "and the marker he was working with was not that shade. It might have been blue, or green. But every mark he made was *that* color. I swear.")

Gradually, Hosea found himself drawing more and more. On Saturdays, on evenings after work. He filled several notebooks full of the scrawling pseudo-letters. Hosea was a very compartmentalized man. He was a creature of routine. He wore the same mechanics' uniform emblazoned with his name, the same dark, steel-toed boots. He always slept in a stocking cap to keep waves in what little hair he had left. He always had a beer after dinner to unwind, and watched *Bonanza*. But, lately, he found himself missing shows, or skipping after-dinner drinks. Sometimes, he would get so involved with his artwork that he was late to meals, or forgot to take the garbage to the curb. Once, he frightened Doreen by getting up in the middle of the night to craft more magenta letters. She saw him with his eyes closed, a beatific expression on his face.

("That's when Mama said it was a cult," Gladys said.)

Hosea and Edna Wray carpooled out to the marsh together later that week. It was their little ritual to a have drink in Olds's silver Airstream. ("A libation for the muse," is how Mrs. Wray put it.) When they drove up, they saw Old Scarecrow standing at the edge of the wetlands, speaking to the empty landscape. He was shirtless and bedraggled looking. Scarecrow's hygiene wasn't a priority at the best of times, but now he looked feral, covered in mud, his unkempt hair free of the cap he usually wore.

The two of them convinced him to come inside and wind down. Hosea walked Scarecrow back to the Airstream and Mrs. Wray set the percolator on to boil coffee.

It took a while for lucidity to come back to Scarecrow. He shivered as Edna and Hosea gently washed him over the sink.

"I don't think he should be out here alone," said Mrs. Wray. "I have an extra room."

The next morning, Hosea drove over to her house before he went to the shop. Old Scarecrow was cleaned up, dressed in one of Mr. Wray's old shirts, and huddled over a cup of coffee.

"How're you doing, Jimmy?" Hosea asked. He sat down next to him.

Scarecrow stared into his coffee, as if it held answers somewhere in its black depths. Finally, he said, "You mind if we move? I can't talk here."

"What do you mean?" Edna Wray asked.

Scarecrow glanced at the curio cabinets full of the dolls. Hosea followed the gaze, and he saw her. The woman in magenta, in miniature. Not painted porcelain and dyed gauze but an actual human female. The dolls' hair was always straight; Wray never altered them. But these dolls all had her hair—wild, wooly, like a bush or a baobab tree. Or like the head of a marsh-bell. Their vivid gowns and veils rippled. The glass eyes were no longer beads of black. They glinted with bistre and hazel notes.

"Let's go into the kitchen," Hosea said, and in saying that, the spell was broken. They were just dolls again, behind a thin glass coffin. They reconvened in the kitchen.

Scarecrow said, "She's destroying my mind. I sleep, and I see her. And when I wake, it's the same. She wants more. More work. More tributes. I can't focus. It's too much."

Edna finally sat down. She was frowning. "She has blessed us. We are *lucky* that we were chosen to spread her message of beauty."

"Well, it sure don't feel like it now," James Olds said. "It feels like a burden. A curse. Every waking hour, she's there. I wish she'd leave me the fuck alone."

When Scarecrow cursed, the pressure seemed to drop in the room. That 'fuck' was as strong as a bomb going off. Edna stood up. Her lips were pressed in a thin line. "Get out," she said. "I won't have profanity in my house."

"Edna, calm down," Hosea said. "I'm sure that Scare—Jimmy didn't mean it. I understand his frustration, though. Lately, she's been eating up more and more of my time. I have a wife and child. And a job. I can't spend all my time with that nonsense."

"I see," said Edna, in a way that suggested that she didn't see at all. "Divinity enters your life, and you just turn it away because it's inconvenient."

"I don't think there's anything 'divine' about the magenta woman. At all." Olds stood up. "I think she's selfish. And vain."

"Out," said Edna Wray.

Hosea drove Scarecrow home, and then he went to work. He stayed out of contact with the coterie and during that time, the visitations and the urges to create lessened. He breathed a sigh of relief, though he missed their camaraderie, and, if he were being honest with himself, the visits to the otherworldly version of Shimmer Marsh.

He made himself forget about the meetings in the marsh, choosing to focus on work. He even went to church for a couple of months. The will-o'-the-wisp orb was simply *ignis fatuus*, or a burp of sulfurous gas.

The shoebox dioramas began appearing in town months after, in random places. One was left in the library, in the children's section. Another on the counter of the coffee shop. They depicted the marsh, and used cellophane Easter grass, blue construction paper, and tiny shells, painted magenta, studding the landscape. People began finding the things in their garages, on their porches, or beneath their decks. Hosea did his best to ignore them. Scarecrow and Edna had probably found another fool to join in their odd rituals.

The Quarles had dinner one evening with the Princes, Charlton and Lorinda. Their daughter Peony was the same age as Gladys, and while they weren't close they were friendly enough. Peony was a frail child, and was allergic to a laundry list of things, including dust, chocolate, strawberries, carrots and milk. Peony was also asthmatic and had to sleep with a nebulizer. As a result of these limiting ailments, Peony did not have many friends. Doreen told Gladys, before they visited the Prince house, "Be sure to be nice to Peony. Try to find something in common."

"I'll try," Gladys said. "But she smells funny. Like medicine and mouthwash."

"Gladys!" Doreen snapped at her. "You be nice!"

There was a sulky nod before they got in the car.

The Prince house was on the opposite side of Shimmer, furthest away from the marsh. Like many of the houses in town, it was a one-story rambler. Charlton had a boat parked in front, alongside a powder blue Ford in pristine shape. Lorinda kept her house immaculately clean. There wasn't a speck of dust anywhere, and the wood furniture was polished to a high gloss. The house was perfumed by the odor of antiseptic cleaning products. Tart lemon and the chemical smell of varnish. Lorinda's hair was a perfect beehive, a molded dome of black hair follicles and hairspray. Charlton's shirt was so stiff with starch that it was a wonder that he didn't cut himself on the sharp angles of his sleeves.

Dinner was simply terrible. Dry chicken cutlets in some kind of beige sauce, probably from a packet. Mashed potatoes without a dash of seasoning. Green beans from a can that had been cooked into a grayish-green sludge. For dessert, there was some kind of brilliant orange gelatin mold that held clouds of cream and maraschino cherries. After dinner, the adults went to the living room where Lorinda and Doreen went to one corner with tiny glasses of sherry and he and Charlton sat opposite them with gin and tonics. The alcohol, at least, was well-mixed. The girls went up to Peony's room.

"Peony showed me her room," Gladys told Xavier. "It looked like a hotel room. The bed was tucked up tight, with hospital corners. You could bounce a penny on it. The carpet looked like office carpet. You know the kind, industrial blue and with no nap whatsoever. There were no toys of any kind. There might have been a book shelf. I don't remember. Everything was so bland and orderly. The fact that the room was showroom-new and neutral made the picture in the room stand out even more.

"Against one wall was the strangest painting I ever saw. It was a painting of a face. It wasn't photo-realistic, mind you. But there was such detail. Like the texture of her skin, or the way her brown eyes had little sparks of gold in them. Her hair was an afro. Back in the late '50s, we thought natural hair was ugly. I don't think I ever saw a woman with unprocessed hair. There were no picks or Afrosheen or 'Black is Beautiful.' In fact, back then, if you called someone Black, those were fighting words. The paper bag test was a real thing back then. 'If you're black, stay back. If you're brown, keep your head down. If you're light, you're all right.' That just the way it was. And in that wild mass of hair, marsh-bells grew, just as if her dark hair was the soil. And that's not all. The marsh-bells seem to glow.

"I was a little thing. Eleven, or twelve. But I recognized that there was some link between that painting and my father's work. Peony told me that her mother had painted it.

"I remember running down to the living room, where the grown-ups were smoking and drinking, and telling Daddy that he had to come to Peony's room. I might have even pulled on his jacket. Mama wasn't too pleased. She thought I was acting up. But I didn't care.

"I don't think I can do justice to the expression on Daddy's face, when he saw the picture. All of the adults came up to look at the painting. Lorinda Prince told Mama that she'd started painting because Edna Wray encouraged her to after she saw Wray's collection of dolls. I don't think Mama liked the painting. I believe she called 'imaginative.' You know, instead of simply saying that it was good. But Daddy…

"He was transfixed. He studied every inch of the painting, down to the paint stroke. He said to Lorinda, 'You see her, too?' Mama frowned. Mr. Prince and Peony looked confused. I forget what Mrs. Prince said, but I remembered the title of the painting. 'Marsh-bell Queen.'

"Daddy burned down the Whitby mansion a week or so later.

"Years later, when Mama was gone to Glory, he told me why he had burned the place. 'The magenta woman, or the Marsh-bell Queen, is made manifest by the act of creation. But once you make her manifest, she infests your brain, fills it with color, and the landscape where she lives. I had to sever that connection somehow.'"

LINC

Once upon a time there lived a boy named Lincoln who lived in a city of white marble mausoleums, and tropical summers. He left his house because he was odd and didn't fit in with his perfect family. They were jewels, sparkling and clear, like diamonds. Lincoln was also a diamond but one with a flaw at his center. This flaw was a dot of color, one that marred his soul.

***

Once upon a time there lived a girl named ____ who lived in a coastal town at the edge of a large marsh. She ran away from her perfect house because she was enslaved but that was not the only reason she ran. She was also odd and didn't fit in with the other slaves. She saw and heard things the others couldn't. Things like: the sound a color made. Or the taste of a shape.

***

When people come into the museum, all of the artwork goes dormant. The muse stops appearing in her woven or painted or sewn vistas. She stops moving and the marsh is frozen. The visitors' gaze is toxic to the muse, and Linc can't help but feel anger at their vacant, lizard-brain stares. They view the work created in her honor as an oddity, a visual freak show. See the two-headed calf, marvel at the bearded lady, see the weird marsh-bell artists. To them, the work of Whitby, Grayson and the others are novel bits of folk art. Not really art per se, but elevated craft. They can't see that the art is a portal to a heavenly dimension, a vision of paradise. To them, the museum is a zoo, and the art on the walls or on pedestals are listless animals. Linc can't help but hate them, as they tramp in with their fanny packs and baseball hats, smelling of fast food and bad coffee. He winces as he hears their sneakered feet squeak on the floor, moving from image to image, gawking, slack-jawed. He knows that most of them think that the work is made by simple-minded Negroes, crude and amateurish and superstitious. They don't think it's Great Art. To them, the Whitby-Grayson Museum is a backwater gallery, a grotesque bit of Americana. They'll roam the former fish-processing plant and then go back to their SUVs, forgetting everything they saw, relegating it to a footnote.

Linc hates these types of visitors, but he tolerates them. The ones he can't stand are the ones like Howard Lenski. The academics. The ones who view the muse as a symbol of some kind, an abstract idea. Not a living thing. The ones who want to pin her down after killing her with ether. They want to dissect her, flay her, and catalog her. He's heard Lenski refer to Shimmer artists as "Art Brut" or "Modern Primitivism." He's overheard groups of visitors say the artwork was created "in the grip of a collective mania." This makes his blood boil, and it's all he can do not to snap at them. Of course, for the most part, neither group can see her, can sense her.

But Xavier is different.

***

The marsh grows on his motel wall. Not the marsh outside, but *her* marsh. Her: the muse. He doesn't know her name. But that doesn't matter. All that matters is her love, and his work.

He started drawing, in permanent marker, on the space above his bed. It's just the outline of things, in black ink that has a strong chemical smell. The Bayside Motel wallpaper was beige and fading. He knew that he'd probably be charged for defacing the property. But he didn't care. Each stroke of the pen bought him in contact with the muse.

***

Violet rage, fuchsia ecstasy.

He's been on the journey from one end of the spectrum to the other. From outcast to acolyte. From darkest purple to hottest pink. The muse shows him the pattern, and in showing it, reveals her own journey.

***

She shows Linc the ship. The dark interior, like a belly, that devoured her father. He lay below her feet, in chains and shit and piss with the other men while the women and children stayed on the deck, under the watchful eyes of the pink men with their guns. She's allowed to wander the deck, because she's so small, but she never does. She stays next to her mother, who holds her and sings in a language that she's forgotten. Once a day, the men are let up on the deck to stretch their legs. When she sees her father, she hardly recognizes him. His skin is ashy and he's thin. His eyes see, but there is no spark of recognition. The men run around the deck, guided by the pink men, and then they go back beneath the deck, to that hollow, hungry place. She shares with Linc:

The air heavy with the smell of salt, fish, algae, sweat, urine, rum, vinegar and unwashed bodies;

The relentless endless expanse of the sea and its tones of blue, green, brown and grey;

The illness that swarms around everyone on the ship, black and brown and pink, the hollow eyes, the curve of scurvy, the bloat of malnutrition, the patches of dry skin and cracked skin, bleeding lips and gums;

The blistering sun that is sometimes red as blood or orange as madness or white as death; the violent storms that streak the sky with whips of lightning;

The powdery taste of hard tack and the stink of salt pork, the blood and guts of the fish that her mother and other womenfolk have to clean;

The sound of the waves as they smash against the hull; the slap as a body is thrown overboard to the waves; the shrill sounds of the pink men's words.

***

"Hey, Howard," Linc says into his phone. "I'm not feeling well today. A stomach thing."

"I think I can manage. Xavier is coming in. Maybe I can put him to work, ha ha," Howard says. "Get better soon."

"Thanks," says Linc.

The outline of the mural is complete. It crawls across wall, pools of water and grassy islets. Cattails and sawgrass. And yes, many marsh-bells waiting to be filled in with color.

A day passes before he realizes that he hasn't eaten. His stomach croaks like a frog, it rumbles like thunder in the marsh. He puts down the pen and markers and the spray paint. She releases him, and fades away. And the world desaturates. Drains of color, of vibrance. His tall, thin lanky body demands food, and sleep. Linc remembers the aftermath of a methamphetamine bender. The crackle-creak of bones. The hazy, humid and waterlogged brain. The distant call of sleep. His body is wrecked. It is a wretched and useless thing, stringy and he can't wait to slough it off, and return to the sacred place.

***

"Are you all right, Mr. White?" Ms. Doshi's voice comes from behind the bullet-proof glass. It takes a moment for her to come into focus, because after the comfortable twilight of his room, the lobby's light is harsh and retina-burning. It's a light that scours out his soul.

She likes natural light.

He blinks Ms. Doshi into focus. The sari she's wearing is a light blue. The color of calm waters. The gentle blue is shot through with gold threads.

"I'm a little under the weather," he manages. His voice sounds wrong. He hasn't spoken in a while.

She steps out from the office. "Is there anything I can do for you?" The concern on her face is genuine. Linc feels embarrassed, and odd. It's been so long since someone gave a shit about him. At least, someone human. She reaches up, and feels his forehead. Her palm is cool, as cool as the blue of her sari.

"You have a fever," Ms. Doshi says. "Come, I'll make you some tea. Have you taken anything for it?"

He opens his mouth. Nothing comes out. His tongue is heavy, with the silt and mud of the marsh. His jaw is a cave full of fish bones and dead plant matter and roots. He follows her, another woman in swirling robes. Robes the wrong color. Everything is the wrong color.

She takes him to the back office and sits him down. He must have fallen asleep because he finds that she's gently nudging him awake. In front of him is a cup of spicy tea, a bottle of aspirin, and a thick slice of a green-tinged cake.

"It's pistachio-white chocolate tea bread," she explains. "You looked hungry. Now, take an aspirin."

He downs a couple of pills with a glass of water that cools his throat. Then he takes a sip of the tea, and Jesus, it's delicious. It's dark and sweet with notes of cardamom and orange. Then he takes a bite of the tea bread. It's so good that he eats the slice in three, maybe four bites. Ms. Doshi brings him two more slices until he's sated.

She sends him back upstairs and tells him to lie down. Linc misses his mother, and thinks about calling her as soon as he gets back to the room. But as soon as he closes the door, he lies down and is out.

***

They file into the room silently, dressed in their best outfits. Women wear dresses made of velvet & lace that sweep the floor, and the men wear suits with starched shirts & ties. There are some women in suits, & a bearded man in a skirt wearing what looks like an

Easter bonnet. They are beautiful. Everyone is beautiful, even the ugly ones, like the man with a harelip or the woman with the large growth on her neck. In here, in this space, the harelip is like a tribal marking, a slash of war paint, & the growth on the woman's neck is a large off-center jewel. The women in suits are handsome, dashing, yet as feminine as they wish to be. The bearded man in the ivory silk dress with a swooping neckline—he was born to wear this dress and that hat with ribbons that disappear into his beard. All of the faces are some shade of brown. All of them wear some article, be it a sash or tie, a jewel or pendant, a boutonniere or a corsage in that wonderful, terrible color. Pink & purple. Purple-pink. Her color. The room they are in is bare, save for some chairs against the walls that form a circle. They all take seats in the circle, as silent as nuns. Then, they start working on various projects. One old black woman with deep-set eyes and hair as white as baking soda works on a doll's dress, sewing the buttons on the front of the tiny garment. A young girl, ten or so, is building some kind of pyramid out of Legos. A middle-aged man with reddish skin and straight, ink-black hair, whittles a piece of wood. All of them are crafters, creating something. Dioramas, models, clothes, jewels. They work with glue, glitter, wire, nail and hammer, cellophane, mylar, gingham. Some of them write, their pens careening over yellow legal pads, vellum, the backs of envelopes, and even speckled composition notebooks. All of them create things—some ugly and primitive, some beautiful and precise—with their eyes closed. Their eyes, behind their shielding lids, move rapidly, as if they are dreaming. Their hands move independently of their bodies, making, creating, piecing together, joining thread and daubing paint. Everything they make has some element of that sacred hue. The pinkpurple, purplepink. Even the music that is played—the bearded man in the gorgeous gown plays a clarinet—even that sounds like that color. This place, this room, it is a Temple. In the center of the circle, a flower begins to manifest. It spills upwards, becomes a kind of robe, and in the center, stands a woman….

***

Someone is calling his name. From far away. "Linc…. Linc…." Is the voice real? Or is it the cry of some bird? Linc can't tell what's real and what isn't. What's marsh and what's Bayside Motel. What's dream and what's painted.

Then comes the frantic knocking and he sullenly pushes the cobwebs of sleep and dream aside and stands up.

"Just a moment," he says.

The room is spinning, and his head feels like it's been swaddled in cotton. But he eventually makes it to the motel room door, and unlocks it.

There stands Xavier. Short, cute as a button Xavier. His tiny pixie dreadlocks like the fronds of some undersea plant, his brow-line glasses.

"Are you okay, man?" he asks. "When you didn't show up for the third day, Howard sent me here."

"It's been three days?" Linc says to himself as much as he does to Xavier. "I…I'm still a little…"

The tarmac of the parking lot begins to blur. He needs to sit down, soon. He sways in the doorframe.

"Whoa, there," Xavier says, as if he were a skittish horse. The thought makes him giggle. "Why don't you sit down," he says, leading him into the room. Linc sits down on the bed.

"Let me get you some—Jesus." Xavier pauses. He's looking at the work on the wall. It's still not complete, but at least the marsh-bells have been colored in. That particular color is easy—she provides it. The other colors—the blues, browns, greens and whites—those he has to mix himself. The piece has grown until it covers the whole wall above his bed.

"Linc. When did you start this mural? Does the motel owner know about it? Why did you—?" The questions come fast and furious, in a volley. He can't answer them all. Or, maybe, he can.

When did you start the mural? I don't know.

Does the motel owner know? I don't care.

Why did you make this? Because of her. For her.

He doesn't say these things aloud. He just sits silently and watches while Xavier takes in the tribute. It wasn't meant for his eyes, but Linc knew that he would be a good acolyte. He might be a better acolyte. Linc had seen some of his artwork online—he'd done some illustrations for a web-based publication. Haunted black and white faces that peered out from pools of water that were overlaid with leaves in autumnal colors.

"Oh, man," says Xavier. "We need to get you to a doctor."

The marsh-bells on the wall begin to glow, like lanterns. Like fireflies and the moon and stars. All in that wonderful, amazing color.

Can't Xavier see it?

Xavier sits next to him, on the bed.

"I don't need a doctor," Linc says. "I just need to sleep."

"Okay. I'll…let you rest. I will check in with you in a few hours." Xavier stands up.

Linc gently pulls him back down. "Stay with me," he says.

***

Two brown bodies blend in the motel room. Fingers and arms become vines, find crevices and nooks. Lips join, tongues entwine. They paint and shape each other, with their hands, and their mouths. Seed and soil and souls join in the magenta glow from the marsh-bells on the wall. Penises become stamens, coiling and entering many different orifices. Semen becomes paint and ink when they both take up brushes and pens and work on the mural that mirrors the marsh surrounding them.

20: ENSEMBLE

Fuchsia

Nights were the worst, when the world drained of color and shape. The child could barely understand the harsh language of the pink demons, and understood their cruelty even less. The food was strange in scent and texture, bland and rubbery. The women were even stranger than the men in their stiff costumes which were little more than cages made of fabric. The rituals were endless, days of sitting on hard benches and singing to the carving of a tortured man who hung in the corner of a dark wooden cavern. The weather of this place was abysmal, blistering days that could swing into torrential downpours at a moment's notice. The morning fogs, the smothering humidity, the stinging biting and burning clouds of insects that were everywhere. The bitter cold that froze the waters of the marsh and killed everything. The horrors of it stretched from horizon to horizon.

But, in spite of it, she loved the land of the pink demons, in a way that they could not see or comprehend.

The daylight hours revealed the beauty of the land. The grass, which was green, brown and yellow. The water, that shimmered in tones of blue and brown and even black. And the flowers in the spring. After the endless palette of the miserable journey—grey, white, brown and endless slate-blue sea—her eyes drank in the color as if she were starved. Rose mallow, purple echinacea, brilliant goldenrod, white asters, all hidden amongst the cordgrass. The butterflies and moths that fluttered among the vegetation were as beautiful as the flowers, white wings threaded with silver or black wings speckled with azure and white. To the child, color was everything. Color was more than just something she saw. The color blue felt like lamb's wool, gentle against her skin. Yellow tasted like sugar. Bright red things made her itch—she avoided looking at cardinals or flowering crimson bee balm. Purple always calmed her. It was the color of peace and the marsh was full of its balm: petunias, phlox, coneflowers, skullcaps and bull thistles were everywhere.

The child's connection to colors almost made her ignore the evil ways of the pink demons. Almost. She saw men with horse bits in their mouths, and raised welts that were rivers of pain trickling down backs. She saw wrists chafed by manacles and fingers blistered by picking tobacco and rice. She heard the pink demons screech out ugly words to those who labored in the sun or in the waterways.

The language of the pink demons was a violent, rough one. Words rasped against her ears. Eventually, she came to understand it. But she would not speak it. The sounds were like burning rocks in her mouth. To listen to it was to hear hatred. To speak it would be corrosive.

They gave her a name, Amarantha, and called her Ama. But mostly they called her nigger, or burr head or little monkey or spook. That was if they noticed her at all. "The little nigglet is mute, and probably feeble-minded," she once overheard a demon say, when she could finally understand their language. Because she was mute and supposedly feeble-minded, her job was to assist the grandmother of the family that owned her.

Fiona MacCubbin was as wrinkled as a sultana, crowned with a feathery storm of white hair. She was a large woman with a red mole that grew hair on the right side of her face. Even her own grandchildren called her the Ogress due to her grotesque appearance. She walked with a cane, both due to her age and to the hammertoes she had. She spoke in an English thickly flavored with her Scottish heritage, with bits of Scots Gaelic slipping through. The Ogress was the nicest of the demons. She called the girl her 'little brownie' and told stories of the Old Country to her. She, too, had once lived by a marsh, and like Ama, had loved and feared it in equal measure.

The marshlands were a magical place. When she got a chance, she would collect shells and feathers to show the Ogress. Mrs. Mac-Cubbin would comment on or ignore her finds; her lucidity varied from day to day. That was when Ama began drawing the things she saw. At first in mud and dust. The Ogress was so enchanted at her 'little sprite's' scribbles that she let her use her supply of ink and paper to practice.

***

Linc's mind was the worst one she had ever been trapped in. The images she saw there terrified her. Even Shadrach loved his strange body more than Linc loved his. The hatred the young man felt for himself was as wide and deep as an ocean. As endless, with many different currents. Nights, he would flay his dream self, and rub salt over the suppurating wounds, so that it was raw and infected. Even the red and yellow exposed mass wasn't enough. His sins flew through its filmy gauze like oil-encased birds, their feathers blackened by noxious chemicals. She saw roach-infested buildings, the floors littered with food and needles. Rooms full of men and women dancing to music that sounded like tea kettle whistles and sheets of metal, dancing not out of joy, but because they had to or else. Low-lit rooms full of antsy manic men, libidos guiding them to each other for frantic couplings. Then there were the crystals that appeared in his dreams. A forest of crystal trees that burned or a river made of the shards. Smoking, snorting and injecting the jagged pieces into his veins. Veins that drained of blood, teeth that rotted in his mouth. The yawning abyss of exhaustion, the hummingbird-quick flashes of euphoria.

Lincoln was possessed by his hatred. He was poisoned by it, as much as the blood in his veins was poisoned. The soil of his soul was rocky, and she couldn't find purchase on it. Then, Ama-Fuchsia remembered the beauty of the marsh-bell, the will-o'-the-wisp. The color of her temporary name. Magenta, fuchsia, purple-pink, pink-purple—that was the color of peace, of sanctuary, of dreams. It was a sacred color. She radiated it through his blasted, twisted inner landscape.

***

In the crucible of Linc's soul, Fuchsia found the name and the life she had discarded and forgotten. When the Ogress died, there had been no need for a mute house slave. They took her artwork away, and sent her to the tobacco fields with its swarm of mosquitoes, click beetles and chiggers, the punishing sun, the hard soil. When she didn't meet her quota, she was punished. No evening supper, and harsh words in that horrible language. The other people who worked alongside her thought she was strange and kept their distance. They thought she was stupid, or devil-touched.

Ama-Fuchsia couldn't remember when she slipped away from the MacCubbin plantation, or what incident had been the catalyst for the escape. She just remembered living in the marsh, moving from islet to forest every day. She'd snatch things from dwellings adjacent to the Shimmer Marsh, food and paper and ink, and abscond into the wetlands, where she could be in the landscape she loved.

She had died at one point or another. Transformed, like water into mist, ice into water.

***

If Lincoln's inner landscape was hell, Xavier's soul was paradise. It was full of color, carefully cataloged. Where Amarantha felt color like a sensation, Xavier examined it, broke it apart into components, and mixed it together. Color was a puzzle to be solved. Ama learned new terminology from Xavier. Hue. Tint. Shade. Lightwave. Spectrum. Prismatic. Palette. Where Lincoln made deformed organic demonic shapes out of his darkness, Xavier constructed elaborate buildings made of color and light, cathedrals and arcades and statues full of careful calculations. She wandered through Xavier's creations, aware that he was trying to define her.

Ignis Fatuus. Eidolon. Ghost. Phantom. Echo. Feral child. Blue light and red light, combined with extra-spectral wavelengths. Marshwoman.

***

She moves between the two of them, between cold mathematical structures and tropical gloom. Soil enriches soil. Soul joins soul. They seed each other, and she seeds them.

Iris

Iris checked Xavier's room. He was still absent. He'd been gone for two nights. His laptop was still there, so she knew that he hadn't left town.

Maybe he and Dr. Lenski hooked up, she thought. She didn't know for a fact that Lenski was gay. But it would have surprised her if he wasn't. Tamar hadn't liked him, for some reason.

"He sucks the energy out of the room," she'd told Iris one time. The aura that surrounded him was dull grey. It had the same texture as industrial carpet. It was like mist, in that it obscured any flare of emotion, or, indeed, personality that he might have had. Iris found him pleasant enough, a cheery and unassuming presence. Tamar visited the Whitby-Grayson Museum at least weekly since it had opened, absorbing the artwork, and the marsh woman's strange influence. Tamar believed Dr. Lenski had a dampening effect. "She's weaker, when he's around," she said. Just before she'd left Shimmer, she called him a "pink demon." It was an odd phrase. Lenski wore pink, that was true. But he was hardly "demonic."

She shuffled back into her room, mildly discomfited. Xavier's aura had become streaked with whorls of magenta. This didn't bother her that much. It was inevitable that something would be stirred up by his research. What did bother her was his affect. He avoided eye contact with her over the week, and mumbled greetings. She told herself that he was just preoccupied with his research, but she couldn't ignore that he had the same distracted quality Tamar had before she went off the rails.

She put these concerns aside, and focused on clearing Tamar's things out of the closet for donation. All of the clothes were ready to go. Iris didn't fit into any of them and she wouldn't have worn them if she had. It would feel weird, as if she were putting on Tamar's skin. There was also a box of her accessories. Bracelets, costume jewelry, and the cloth flowers she pinned to her hair. Toward the end, Tamar had only worn the cloth marsh-bells Iris had made. She kept one, and considered adding it to the pile.

Iris remembered making the flowers out of tulle, silk, nylon and wire. Each micro-blossom was hand rolled and meticulously affixed to the center of a wool felt ball with tiny beads of glue. The work required precision, and she frequently pricked her fingers. But none of that mattered. The blood drops, or the pain. Because while she worked, she was in that dream sanctuary, in Fuchsia's presence. It was addictive. She would lose hours, and sometimes, a whole day in that becalmed place. Fuchsia's marsh was better than the real Shimmer Marsh. The colors there were more intense. The cries of the marsh birds painted the sky. The gulls' bleat made clouds, cirrus wisps. Frog croaks grew silver mists. The great blue heron was the color of the water, seemed to be made of it, and the black and red ibis's curved beak was like a pen, etching the landscape into existence.

Iris came to a decision. She would get rid of the lone cloth marshbell. It was a trigger. It was one more thing that reminded her of Tamar.

Her cellphone beeped, interrupting her reverie. It beeped a couple of more times as she fumbled it out of her pocket.

They were text messages from a 202 area code, so they were probably from Xavier. She swiped until she reached the messages, finding a series of pictures rather than words. The pictures showed a mural crawling across a wall. Each picture, four in total, dripped with color, green-gold, wet blue, and blazing magenta. The third picture was one of those panorama shots, where you could spin the view around.

The fourth picture was a picture of the marsh woman. The dark muse. Someone—Xavier?—had painted her. Her trademark robes were made of a thousand tiny blossoms. The blossoms were also entwined in her braided hair. She floated above the landscape, a nature goddess. Our Lady of the Marsh. She radiated with power, like Oya and Yemaya. The painting—or drawing—was outlined with a glowing aura. Iris wasn't sure if the aura had been painted or if it was, indeed, an aura.

Her examination of the fourth picture was interrupted by a fifth message. This one was a video. It showed a tall, gaunt man filling in more of the painting with his fingers. The video was short, maybe five seconds, but she recognized the location. The rickety light from the Bayside Motel glowed through the curtain, competing with the magenta light.

Iris called the number. It went to voicemail. She called the number again and again, seven times. The eighth time, it picked up. She heard voices, Xavier's and another guy's, in the distance, along with the cries of gulls. She said Xavier's name a few times, but it was obvious that he wasn't listening.

The muse was summoning him, as she had once summoned her.

Iris found herself getting her car keys.

***

"She is alive in me," Tamar told her on that day, five years ago. It had been late April and the heavy rains had just stopped. The trees had begun to bud, and new grass sprouted. They had driven to the edge of the Shimmer Marsh, because Tamar wanted to collect some marsh flowers to use in her new creations. They gathered larkspur, foxglove, phlox and rose mallow blossoms. Animals watched as the women reaped the shores, circling gulls and wading herons.

Iris found Tamar on the kitchen floor earlier that week, along with hundreds of images cut out from magazines, bottles of glue and discarded scraps. Tamar was a mess, sweating and wild-eyed as she cut out figures and sorted them. Iris watched her unobserved for a while, both intrigued and disturbed. She saw Tamar murmur as she worked, placing various images here and there on pasteboard, as if she were arranging a puzzle.

Then, Iris stopped her. She took the scissors away, and gently pulled her away from the chaos. Tamar had looked crazed then. Her hair, usually so carefully styled, was chaotic with random braids, stray glitter and petals. She stopped her because Tamar had never looked so beautiful. Her skin was the color of river clay, rich and brown. The freckles were dark silt scattered across her body. Tamar had become the angel of the marsh. They had sex then. Ugly, feral, devouring sex. They writhed there, among the brushes, paper and images of flowers and the faces of black women. Their bodies blended, and the marsh waters rose flooding them.

Iris was almost washed away by it all. Images flashed in her brain. The marsh populated by brilliant flowers. Flowers that became people who endlessly built the marsh out of yarn, paint, ink, tile. Tamar was one of their number, placing a bird in the flawless blue sky, shaping a cattail reed. The rush of euphoria filled her, then. She wanted to be there, forever. To finally belong somewhere. This timeless, placeless place was paradise. She felt, rather than saw, the muse or angel nearby. She was an orchid, feeding on the dreams of the outcast.

"That wasn't you, was it?" Iris said, at the edge of the marsh. The ruin of the Whitby mansion lingered on the bank behind them, reclaimed by nature. "When we…. A few days ago."

"I don't know where she ends, and I begin," Tamar said. "I have to leave this place. Or I'll drown. That's what she does, Iris. She fills your head with such beauty, such color that you have to get it down somehow. And you want to, too. To her, color is sacred. It's life itself."

"You can resist it," Iris replied after a while.

"No," Tamar said. "*You* can resist her. I cannot. Neither could the others."

***

AMARANTHA

The two men were dark and light, or colors that clashed. Lincoln was mud and dark, and his chthonic secrets blistered beneath his skin. Xavier was the glitter of light on water, cool water on tortured skin. Lincoln was the wound, and Xavier was the salve.

Her time slithering in Lincoln's soul gave her back her name, and the shape of her life. It was something she wanted to forget, and leave behind. She knew she had died in the marsh, probably from exposure to the cold. In Xavier's soul, her story was transformed into abstract patterns, like houndstooth or damask silk. Her pain and confusion and voicelessness were designs or textures.

She echoed back and forth between the two men as they completed the wall mural.

More green here, less blue there. Capture the bite of razor grass, the speckles of algae, the iridescence of a moth's wing. Xavier sketched the shapes—the creatures, the sediment, the rocks, the tufts of grass. Linc filled them in with color. What colors he lacked in his meager palette, bought at some hardware store, she supplied. Honeygreen. Crimsonwhite. Beetleblack. Aquasilver. With each stroke, they painted the world of her dreams.

***

Iris

When Iris pulled into the Bayside Motel parking lot, she felt like a fool. How was she going to find the right room? The motel was a glorified motor lodge, a relic from the 1960s. She guessed, but did not know that the thin, tall maintenance man from the Whitby-Grayson Museum might live here temporarily, but she didn't recall his name. Was it Logan, or Lawrence? It was an L name. But she couldn't very well go to the office with that little information.

She scrolled through her pictures to see if maybe there were some clues in the videos and pictures Xavier had sent.

Neither the video nor the pictures were there.

"No fucking way," she said aloud. Mona Broome would have not approved of her unladylike cussing. Neither would Pop-Pop.

Heaven sounded like one bland, boring place. Vanilla, and not the artisanal kind, either. She shooed the thought away, with a bitter laugh. She had seen the pictures, and heard her phone beep twenty minutes ago. She had *not* imagined it. Yet here she was, in a run-down motel parking lot, feeling like a fool.

The motor was still running. She moved her steering wheel—

The fuchsia flashed in the corner of her eye. She turned to her right, and saw it. A ball of glowing light, like a hovering Christmas ornament, floated toward the motel lazily. The gaseous sphere of flame drifted up, up to the second floor railing and hovered in front of one of the doors with moth-like quiescence.

Iris let her mind go dormant. She tried her best to tamp down any emotion she felt. She felt it anyway. Dread, tinged with excitement. It grew in her chest, nearly as bright as the will-o'-the-wisp. She was certain that she was going to see something amazing. Something wonderful, something terrible. It didn't matter which one.

She turned off her car. She was up the stairs before she realized it. *Did I lock my car? Did I lock the door to my house?*

She found that she didn't care.

She knocked on the maroon door.

***

Amarantha

The wall glowed when the woman entered the room. It glowed with the stuff of her soul. The mural was almost complete. The grass shivered though there was no wind. The sky was brilliant blue though there was no sun. The water rippled, and the birds flew. She named the things in the marsh on the wall. Paw Paw. Osprey. Blue crab.

Amarantha was tired. Her flame was fading. She had been away from the dream world for too long. It felt like forever. For too long, she had wandered, trapped in the minds and souls and dreams of broken people. Her most recent two acolytes were also tired, souls worn smooth. They could work no more. She was almost home. Almost. But something was missing.

The third acolyte had arrived just in time to finish the mural.

Iris moved over Xavier and Linc, who huddled together on the motel bed, and picked up a brush.

She added words in one corner of the mural.

ACKNOWLEDGMENTS

Thanks to the Wyrd Words crew, who saw earlier drafts of this novel: Valya Lupescu, Stephen Segal, Jason Heller, Sam J. Miller, Scott Woods, Eric San Juan, Mary Anne Mohanraj, John Klima, Emily Jiang, R.K. Kalaw, Bo Bolander, K. Tempest Bradford.

To Word Horde/Ross Lockhart for taking on this project.

And finally, to the Outer Dark community, for their support.

"At once sly and grim, soberingly real and darkly fantastical, the story of the Waite sisters will haunt readers like an eerie old folk song."
—*Publishers Weekly (starred review)*

When newscaster Abby Waite is diagnosed with a potentially terminal illness, she decides to do the logical thing... break her twin sister Martha out of prison and hit the road. Their destination is the Waite family cabin in Minnesota where Abby plans a family reunion of sorts. But when you come from a family where your grandfather frequently took control of your body during your youth, where your mother tried to inhabit your mind and suck your youthful energies out of you, and where so many dark secrets—and bodies, even—are buried, such a family meeting promises to be nothing short of complicated...

Trade Paperback, 268 pp, $16.99

ISBN-13: 978-1-939905-46-8

http://www.wordhorde.com

"Hauser delivers an engrossing, baffling horror debut that veers hard into the weird, its disturbing aspects enhanced by its faux-nonfictional structure."

—*Publishers Weekly*

Underground filmmaker Tina Mori became a legend in the late 1970s with a stolen camera, a series of visionary Super 8 shorts and a single feature film, heralded as her masterpiece, *Dragon's Teeth*. Then she disappeared under mysterious circumstances…

Through many layers, including letters, a 'zine made by a teenage horror film fan, and a memoir written by Mori's college roommate and muse, film historian and debut novelist Brian Hauser delves deep into Tina Mori's life and legacy, exploring the strange depths and fathomless shadows situated between truth, fiction, fantasy, and the uncanny.

Format: Trade Paperback, 260 pp, $16.99

ISBN-13: 978-1-939905-48-2

http://www.wordhorde.com

ABOUT THE AUTHOR

Craig Laurance Gidney is the author of the collections *Sea, Swallow Me & Other Stories* (Lethe Press, 2008), *Skin Deep Magic* (Rebel Satori Press, 2014), the Young Adult novel *Bereft* (Tiny Satchel Press, 2013) and *The Nectar of Nightmares* (Dim Shores, 2015). His work has been nominated for the Lambda Literary and Gaylactic Spectrum Awards, and he has won both the Bronze Moonbeam and Silver Independent Publishers Book Awards. He lives in his native Washington, DC. Website: craiglaurancegidney.com. Instagram, Tumblr & Twitter: ethereallad.